TEQUILA'S SUNRISE

BRIAN KEENE

deadite
press

deadite
press

DEADITE PRESS
205 NE BRYANT
PORTLAND, OR 97211
www.DEADITEPRESS.com

AN ERASERHEAD PRESS COMPANY
www.ERASERHEADPRESS.com

ISBN: 1-936383-55-1

Acknowledgements

For this new edition of *Tequila's Sunrise*, my thanks to everyone at Deadite Press; Alex McVey; Dallas Mayr (whose The Transformed Mouse inspired this tale); Tod Clark, Kelli Owen, Mark Sylva, and John Urbancik (who proofread the original version); Geoff Cooper; Mike Oliveri; Mikey Huyck; J. F. Gonzalez; Mary SanGiovanni; and my sons.

OTHER DEADITE PRESS BOOKS BY BRIAN KEENE
Urban Gothic
Jack's Magic Beans
Clickers II (with J.F. Gonzalez)
Take The Long Way Home
A Gathering of Crows
Darkness on the Edge of Town

For Dave Thomas: "Para todo mal, mescal. Para todo bien, también." *(For all hardships, mezcal. For all wellness, as well.)*

CONTENTS

TEQUILA'S SUNRISE

(A FABLE)

Tequila has no history; there are no anecdotes confirming its birth. This is how it's been since the beginning of time, for tequila is a gift from the gods and they don't tend to offer fables when bestowing favors. That is the job of mortals, the children of panic and tradition.
—Alvaro Mutis

Where shall I go?
Where shall I go?
The road of the god of duality.
Is your house in the place of the fleshless?
Perchance inside heaven?
Or here on earth only?
—Traditional Aztec funeral chant

To open doors, one must first know how to find them.
—Daemonolateria

Once upon a time, which is how most fables begin, there was a land known as Oaxaca. The people who lived in Oaxaca called themselves the Tenochas, but history would call them the Aztecs. Oaxaca was a deadly place, a country full of extremes—in its people, creatures, and the landscape itself. Although it offered much beauty and wonder, there were myriad dangers lurking there, as well.

Atop one of Oaxaca's snow-covered, treeless mountains, a thousand feet above the sea and overlooking a wide, fertile valley, sat the city of Monte Alban. It was a large city (though not the biggest) and many people lived there. In the morning, the sun glinted off the frescoed temples and buildings in its plaza. At night, the moon reflected on its ceremonial pools.

Before the Spaniards arrived in Oaxaca, a young boy named Chalco could often be found on Monte Alban's expansive ball courts playing tlachtli and patolli with his friends. But when Cortes's army landed on their shores, Lord Moctezuma issued a war summons. The invaders' intentions were unclear. They said they came in peace, but they brought a new god and drove the people of Oaxaca before them like cattle.

11

Most of the able-bodied men in Monte Alban answered Moctezuma's call to arms, and traveled to the capital city of Tenochtitlan. Chalco and the other boys had to assume their place and were now responsible for farming, hunting, and all the other tasks. There was no more time for play or fun—only for the everyday drudgery of life. Childhood ended early and there was no time to miss it or weep for its passing. There were no more games and no more play, and the ball courts sat empty and silent, their stones dusty.

Some people said it was the end of the world.

Perhaps they were right.

The day Chalco met the worm began like any other.

It began in darkness.

Before dawn, the call to rise echoed across the city, as it did every day. Inside the pyramid temples, the priests blew conch shell trumpets while their acolytes beat on wooden drums. The noise disturbed the birds roosting on the temple peaks. Shrieking, they flew into the sky, adding to the cacophony. The music throbbed through the streets and alleys, waking the residents.

Chalco stared up at the thatched roof of his family's adobe hut and rubbed sleep dust from the corners of his eyes. He was still tired. After working in the fields all day long, he'd gone to bed late the night before. Today would offer a welcome change. He planned on going hunting. His clan's larder grew empty.

The drumming continued and the trumpets sounded again. Around him, Chalco's mother, sisters, and younger brother stirred. The adobe had two rooms, partitioned down the middle. On one side were the sleeping quarters. The other side held the kitchen and dining area. As Chalco stumbled out of bed, his mother tended to the fire, which they'd banked the night before. Kneeling, she blew it back to life. Was it his imagination or did she look older today than she had in recent months? Her once black hair was now streaked with white. She didn't smile very much anymore, and there were lines on her face. He knew that she missed his father. Chalco missed him, too. He wondered if they'd see him again.

Outside, the trumpets sounded one more time—wailing long and mournfully before they faded. Somewhere, in a nearby hut, a baby cried.

Yawning, Chalco got dressed. He passed his otterskin maxtli between his legs, and then cinched it around his waist. The two ends of the loincloth hanging down in the front and back were embellished with intricate designs of an eagle and a jaguar—the totems of his clan. He pulled a mantle of woven cloth over his left shoulder, and then slipped into his deerskin sandals. His feet had gotten bigger, and his toes felt cramped inside them. Soon, it would be time for a new pair. At five feet five inches, Chalco was considered tall for his people. His father often joked that perhaps he was really the son of the cannibal giants rumored to live in the Northern caves. But he also said that Chalco's size was a blessing, especially when it came to work. His broad head and thick neck were good for carrying baskets, and his long, muscular arms and wide feet aided him both in the field and on the hunt. Chalco did not mind his size. He knew it gave him an advantage over the other boys. The only thing he did not like was his coarse, dark hair. Currently, the thick bangs hung over his almond-shaped eyes and got in his way. He had to constantly flip his hair away from his face. Despite the annoyance, Chalco was reluctant to cut it. He wanted a long, braided ponytail like many of the older men had. He'd noticed that women seemed to fancy them.

The fire's glow filled the hut. The warmth felt good. Dressed for the day, Chalco turned to his little brother. He was still in bed, blinking, half-awake.

"Quintox, get up."

The younger boy shook his head. "I am still tired, Chalco."

"Did you not rest well?" Chalco knew that Quintox missed their father and uncles, and wondered if it was affecting his sleep.

"I had a strange dream."

Chalco sat on the edge of the bed and patted his head. "What was it?"

"I shouldn't say." Quintox frowned. "It might be wrong to tell."

"Then whisper if you are ashamed, so that our sisters won't hear."

Quintox lowered his voice. His eyes were wide. His bottom lip trembled. "I dreamed that Cortes was really Quetzalcoatl."

Chalco stiffened. He glanced around quickly, making sure the rest of the family hadn't heard his brother's blasphemy. Such talk could lead to only one thing—Quintox being sacrificed to Tlaloc, the rain god who required children several times a year as tribute. Although the priests also gathered children's tears in a ceremonial bowl as an offering, that would not be Quintox's fate. Not for blasphemy. He would shed blood rather than tears. To compare Quetzalcoatl, the Plumed Serpent, greatest of all the gods, to Cortes, the leader of the Spanish invaders, was unforgivable.

"Stop that right now. I mean it. No more of this talk."

"But Chalco, the priests say that this is the year Quetzalcoatl is supposed to return. Remember? He promised that he would come back and deliver us. He would usher in a new era of peace and prosperity. 'Look to the east', they say. If this is the end of the world, then surely he must come."

The boy recited it from memory. The prophecy was ingrained in them all from the time they learned to speak and read. Chalco knew it well. In Tenochtitlan's grandest place of worship—a temple devoted to Tonatiuh, the sun god—there was a gigantic stone monolith, eighteen feet in diameter and carved from a single, black volcanic rock. It was a calendar. According to the calendar, Quetzalcoatl would return this year to save his faithful servants. He would sail across the ocean from parts unknown and arrive on Oaxaca's eastern shore. After he'd driven their enemies from the land, one hundred years of peace would follow. So far, none of this had come to pass. Instead of Quetzalcoatl, it had been Cortes and his armies who landed on the eastern shore. They'd carved a swath through the country as they pressed farther inland, claiming to come in peace even while people died. It was a bad omen.

Although he would never admit it out loud, Chalco often wondered if Quetzalcoatl would ever return. Maybe the priests were wrong. Or maybe… maybe the plumed serpent didn't even exist. Maybe none of the gods did. Perhaps the gods were just stories. It wasn't the first time he'd considered this, and it filled him with dread. In the light of day, he was sure the gods

14

existed, and fearful they would exact revenge for his doubt.

"Chalco," Quintox asked. "What are you thinking?"

"Nothing." Ashamed by his thoughts, Chalco pulled the covers off his little brother and boxed the boy's ears. "Enough talk. The sun will be up before you are. Get dressed. And don't speak of this anymore."

When Quintox was ready, they kissed their mother goodbye and walked down the street to the communal bathhouse. The huts were separated—one for men and one for women. The boys took their place in line and slowly shuffled forward. Once inside, they undressed and then bathed, using sticky soap made from tree sap. Morose slaves poured water over heated rocks and the room filled with steam. As they cleaned themselves, the boys listened to the older men gossip—merchants, craftsmen, medicine doctors, priests, the elderly or infirm, and others who had been excused from Moctezuma's call to arms.

The talk was mixed; much of it was dire. A black pheasant had been spotted the day before, lurking in the brush near the temple of Huehueteotl. A prisoner of war, condemned to sacrifice, briefly lived after his head was cut from his body. His legs and arms had flopped and jittered while the priest held his severed head aloft. Then his decapitated body tried to run away. Another priest who'd been carrying a stone tray laden with palpitating human hearts had been wounded by a jaguar. The beast leapt from the shadows and mauled the unfortunate victim, and then snatched the offerings from the tray before vanishing. A two-headed calf was born in the night. It cried out like a human and then died. A metalworker came in contact with his wife's menstrual blood—always an invitation to disaster.

Bad tidings, all.

To make matters worse, these things happened in the midst of an invasion. The Spanish continued with their conquest, and the talk and rumors soon turned to that. It was said they brought their own slaves with them—people with skin as black as coal. The men in the steam room wondered what kind of people these obsidian slaves were. They seemed fierce and proud. Could they not rise up against their captors and break their bonds?

When they'd finished bathing, the boys got dressed again and hurried home for a breakfast of tortillas, beans, and warm goat's milk. In contrast to the gossip of the bathhouse, Chalco's family ate in silence. His mother admonished one of his sisters to chew with her mouth closed. Quintox asked for more beans. But other than that, they were quiet. Their mood mirrored the oppressive atmosphere that seemed to hang over all of Monte Alban.

After breakfast was finished, his mother and sisters cleaned the clay bowls while Chalco drew his brother aside.

"I must go hunting today. We need more meat."

Quintox grew excited. "Can I come with you? Please? Before he left, Father said that I am old enough to start learning how to hunt."

"And you are." Chalco smiled. "Soon, I'll teach you as Father taught me. But not today. There is too much to be done. Mother needs help in the fields—you have a strong back, just like I do. Just like all the men in our clan. You will be more help to us there."

Quintox's expression soured. He looked at the ground and pouted.

"But I don't want to farm. Farming isn't noble or exciting. I want to hunt—to help."

"Listen." Chalco squeezed his shoulder. "It's war time. We each have to do our part. That is the way it has always been. Remember what we've been taught. Nobody is more important than another, except for Lord Moctezuma and the priests. By helping our mother in the fields you are helping us all. That is a very noble thing, Quintox—the noblest thing of all. Honor our clan. And don't worry. There will be many more days to go hunting, and much game to kill. You'll get your chance."

"Promise?"

"I promise."

Quintox smiled. "I want to grow up just like you. I want to make our father proud, the way you do."

"Oh, you do, Quintox. You really do. You make our entire clan very proud."

And he did. Chalco had very recently begun to take an interest in girls, particularly Yamesha, the jewel-cutter's

16

daughter. He hoped that when the time came, their families might arrange a marriage for them. If so, he hoped that his first child would be a son—and that the boy would be just like his little brother.

Grinning, he gently boxed Quintox's ears. The younger boy pushed him away. Laughing, they punched one another until their mother spoke up. Her voice was stern and tired.

"Go on now, both of you. Enough talking. You can do that at dinnertime. To the fields with you, Quintox. The sun is coming up. It will be hot in a few hours. It is better to work now, while the air is still cool."

"Are you not coming, Mother?" Quintox asked.

"I will join you shortly. First, I must stop by the temple and offer prayers for your father and uncles. Chalco, your sisters have prepared a lunch for you to take on the hunt. Don't forget it."

"Thank you, Mother. I won't."

She kissed them both and then left the hut. Quintox and his sisters departed for the fields. Alone in the dwelling, Chalco gathered his weapons. He strapped a deer hide sheath to his waist and thrust his stone knife into it. Then he collected his bow and strapped a quiver of arrows over his back. Finally, he slung a wicker basket over his other shoulder. Inside were tortillas, wrapped in leaves to keep them fresh, along with two small limes and a water skin sealed with beeswax. The skin was filled with pulque, a slightly alcoholic drink made from agave. Chalco preferred water. He hated the bitter taste of pulque. But it would give him stamina later, and water was too precious to spare. Rain had been scarce this season and water was being rationed.

Chalco departed. The first rays of dawn shone across the sky. With many of the men off to war, the streets were quieter than normal. But in the silence, Chalco heard things he didn't normally pay attention to. Birds chirped from the rooftops, having returned to their roosts once the morning trumpets faded. A goat snorted as Chalco passed by a trough. A baby wailed from a nearby hut. In one of the temples, the first sacrifice of the day screamed. Several small children chased each other in the street, shrieking in delight. The cries intermingled, becoming

17

indistinguishable from one another—screams or laughter, they sounded the same.

Chalco admired one of the pyramids as he passed by. He wished, not for the first time, that he could build something like it. How grand would that be, to honor the gods and his clan in such a manner? But his skills lay elsewhere, like his father and his father before him. He was a hunter and a farmer— and a warrior. His hands were made for soil and blood, rather than stone and brick. Still, he'd always been enamored with Monte Alban's artisans and craftsmen. The city's architecture was marvelous. Chalco hoped that one day soon he might travel to the capital, and gaze upon Tenochtitlan's fountains and immaculately clean streets. He'd heard so many wonderful stories about the city. They had running water there. The temples were supposed to be the grandest in all of Oaxaca. He longed to traverse the canals, visit the great houses full of books, to touch the golden Codex wheel, and see Lord Moctezuma's procession as they passed by adorned with bells and jewels and brightly colored feathers. It was said that dancers went before him, casting flower petals on the ground. Chalco thought that it must be a magnificent sight. Perhaps the greatest in all the world.

Chalco shuddered, wondering what would happen to all of Tenochtitlan's wonders if they fell into the invaders' hands. Would Monte Alban be next? If so, what would happen to his clan? His family? To his little brother? To Yamesha? The thought made his stomach hurt. Around the next corner, he passed an old woman pushing a cart piled high with woven fabrics. The old woman did not smile. He knew how she felt.

Gripping his bow tightly, Chalco clenched his teeth and walked on. He passed by a row of stone monuments—a throne symbolizing Moctezuma's rule, and several giant heads representing the previous rulers. Slaves scrubbed bird droppings from the carvings. They hummed as they worked. The tune was sad.

When he arrived at the marketplace, the city came to life, bustling with sound and activity. Voices cried out between the stalls, bartering and selling, and alternately praising or beseeching Yacatecuhtli, the god of merchants. The market thrummed with smells and sights. There was livestock and wild game: rabbits, lizards, serpents, quail, partridges, turkeys, pigeons, parrots, and goats—some alive and others freshly killed. He ignored these, thankful as always that he came from a clan of hunters. There was no need to spend money on such things when you could kill it yourself.

Flipping his bangs away from his eyes, Chalco passed by a row of apothecaries. In front of the structures, merchants sold medicinal herbs and roots, as well as charms and totems. There was a barbershop, a rug-maker, and a metalworker. On a small platform, sullen slaves—mostly the children of other slaves or prisoners of war from beyond Oaxaca's borders—were sold like livestock. Sometimes, Chalco felt sorry for the slaves. But they were necessary. Prostitutes preened in a side-alley, ready to start another day. With so many of the men gone, their business was down. Craftsmen shouted, hawking their various wares and services. There were stalls of cotton, thread, sandals, animal skins, blankets, dyes, pottery, ceramic dolls, trinkets, amulets, rope, bricks and mortar, oils, paints, charcoal, beads, paper, tobacco, salt, gold, silver, precious stones like jade and amber, feathers and quetzal plumes, earrings and nose ornaments, weapons, tackle, wicker baskets, and even imported lumber (since Monte Alban had sparse woodlands).

Chalco's mouth watered as he passed by maize, beans, maguey, peppers, cereals, squash, sweet potatoes, pumpkins, tomatoes, nuts, and chocolate. If the hunt was bountiful, he would sell some wild game on his return and buy some chocolate for his mother and siblings. That would make them happy. For the first time since his departure, Chalco smiled.

He reached the outskirts of the city and passed through the fields. Clan members and slaves worked alongside each other, tending rows of maize and beans, and gathering tree sap to make rubber and soap. An apiary buzzed with honeybees. Smoke curled from a burning sewage pit. A group of warriors— left behind to guard Monte Alban when the rest of the men had gone—wound their way along a narrow trail, traveling down into the valley below. Their faces were grim, their bodies painted. Chalco wondered where they were going, but didn't ask.

After slinging his bow with gut-thread and readjusting his quiver and basket, Chalco headed farther up the mountain. It was easy travel at first. He stuck to the well-trod footpath, avoiding the prickly cacti. Soon, the city's noise faded and the sounds of nature took over—the screech of a hawk far overhead (out of range of his arrows), the whisper of a spider clambering over a rock, a bush rustling in an all too- brief gust of wind. He saw no other people and no game, either. The countryside was deserted. The hot sun climbed higher into the sky and no further breezes were forthcoming. Chalco started to sweat. Thin beads of perspiration dripped from his forehead and upper lip. The steep, winding trail grew narrower, and then vanished altogether. Chalco pressed on, watching where he stepped, alert for snakes and scorpions. Both could penetrate the soles of his sandals. There was still no movement. He found some rabbit tracks in the dirt, but they were at least two days old. A sidewinder track followed after them. He wasn't the only predator looking for game. He hoped the serpent had better luck than him.

The bow grew slippery in his sweaty hands. He spotted a brown lizard sunning itself on a flat stone, but it was too small to bother with—nothing more than a mouthful. It skittered away as he walked by. Pausing, Chalco knelt in the dirt and rooted through his basket. He pulled out the water skin, unsealed the beeswax with his thumbnail, and took a long drink of pulque, grimacing at the taste. Then he sealed it back up and pulled a lime from the basket. Continuing on his way, he bit a hole in the fruit, relishing the tangy peel. He sucked the juice out as he walked. Sweat ran into his eyes. Even this far from Monte Alban, the mountain still seemed deserted. It was as if all the wildlife had fled from the advancing Spaniards.

Boredom set in and instead of watching for game, Chalco daydreamed. He thought of his friends. He remembered their days spent playing tlachtli, or gathering in the main plaza to watch prisoners of war be sacrificed, or joining in the great feasts. He missed his friends. They rarely saw each other these days. Like him, their fathers had all gone to Tenochtitlan and the boys were left to provide for their clans. The only time he really got to see his friends anymore was at temple, and then they couldn't speak freely.

His thoughts turned to Yamesha, and his stomach fluttered. More sweat stung his eyes, but now it wasn't just from the heat. He hated the way Yamesha made him feel, but at the same time, it excited him. On the rare occasions that he got to talk with her, Chalco's mouth refused to work. He tried hard to think of something clever or funny to say. Instead, he said nothing. When she looked at him, he looked away. When she smiled at him, he frowned. Yet she was never far from his thoughts. She was intoxicating—and terrifying. The worst part was that he didn't understand why. What made the jeweler's daughter so different than the other women in his life? His sisters didn't have that effect on him. Neither did his mother or aunts. Why should it be otherwise with Yamesha? Why should he grow his hair long just to impress her? It made no sense.

Despite his conflicted emotions, Chalco really did want to marry her. At fourteen, he wasn't old enough yet. Men from the clans could marry at twenty and the women at sixteen. But with all of the recent changes in Monte Alban, perhaps the priests would ease that restriction. After all, if, in his father's absence, Chalco was now the head of his clan, why could he not enjoy all the benefits of adulthood? Couldn't he and Yamesha perform the right of Tilmantli, just like any other young couple? They were of different clans and different blood, as required by law. That was enough. He pictured himself going before the clan council and seeking permission from the old woman matchmaker.

His father was there, celebrating victory over the invaders. His mother was smiling again, as were his sisters. So was Quintox.

I want to be just like you…

Lost in his fantasies, Chalco didn't see the pheasant lurking inside a nearby thicket. Startled by his approach, the bird burst from the shrubs, squawking with fright. Its wings beat the air in an explosion of multi-colored feathers. Startled, Chalco jumped backward, dropping his bow. His heart beat faster. As the pheasant flew away, he scrambled to retrieve the weapon. He notched an arrow with trembling hands and tried to aim, but the bird was already out of range.

"Gods damn the fowl!" Chalco shivered, and then

wondered why. It was the middle of the day. The sun was at its peak. He should be sweltering in the heat. Instead, his sweat had dried on his skin.

He glanced around, stunned. There were no familiar landmarks, no rockslides or canyons or caves that he recognized. Lost inside his head, thoughts consumed with Yamesha, he had wandered farther up the mountain than he'd ever been before. But how? Had he really been daydreaming that long? It didn't feel like it. He pushed his hair back and looked up at the sun again. It was in the midday position. Impossible. How could he have wandered for so long, without falling into a chasm or tripping over a stone? How had he made it so far without coming to harm? Surely, the gods had watched over him. Had they guided him here, as well?

His shock gave way to curiosity. An overwhelming sense of adventure stirred inside him. If the gods had indeed guided him here, he reasoned, there must be a purpose behind it. He decided to explore farther. If anything, perhaps the wildlife would be more plentiful here. As long as he didn't kill anything too heavy—like a wolf or a deer— he shouldn't have trouble hauling it back to Monte Alban.

After washing down his lunch with a sip of pulque, Chalco pressed on. Slinging his bow over his back, he scaled a small cliff, his agile fingers expertly finding the right cracks. He jumped over a deep crevice. A jaguar's skeleton lay at the bottom, bleached bones pointing towards the mountaintop. He paid his clan's totem animal a silent tribute. The air grew colder, the vegetation more sparse. Soon, his sandals crunched over a thin layer of snow. There were tracks in the frost—rabbit, coyote, and deer. Un-slinging the bow again, he notched an arrow, proceeding up the mountain with caution, his senses alert for any movement or sound.

He clambered up onto a small jumble of boulders and paused, staring back down at the city, and the valley far below it. A shimmering haze seemed to hang over Monte Alban. The buildings and pyramids seemed so small from this height, like tiny replicas rather than real structures.

"It is beautiful," he whispered.

"Yes, it is."

Chalco screamed.

"Oh, stop that," the voice said. "You'll scare everything away and have to return home empty-handed tonight."

Chalco whirled around. He was alone, yet the speaker sounded like they were right beside him. It was a male voice, deep and calm, almost hypnotic. He scanned the mountainside. There was nothing to hide behind. The nearest boulder was too far away, and the only plants were a few thin, scraggly pines and a single agave plant. He was momentarily surprised to see an agave growing this far up the mountain, but before he could consider it further, the voice spoke again.

"Look again, Chalco. Look at your home."

"W-who are you? Where are you?"

"I am one of the first. I am everywhere and in between. I am here with you."

Chalco turned around in a circle, trying to find the source. The voice sounded like it was coming from four different directions at once.

"Y-you speak Nahuatl?" he asked.

"No," the voice said. "You hear Nahuatl. I speak the language of my kind."

"Are y-you a…god?"

Chalco's voice was barely a whisper. In contrast, the other speaker laughed loudly. The sound boomed across the mountain, echoing off the rocks. Chalco began to tremble. Unable to hold the bow steady, he slung it over his back and drew his knife. Then he dropped into a defensive stance and held the weapon in front of him. This was no god. Surely it was a demon, or perhaps one of the giants his father spoke of. It would try to eat him if he didn't fight it off. But where was it? The laughter faded. Silence returned.

"Please," Chalco cried. "Please, demon. I have done nothing to you. If I am trespassing in your domain, then I am sorry. I was merely hunting and then—"

"Do not be afraid. I am no demon. Your first guess was right, even though it is such a small word. Although I am not a god in the true sense, your kind considers me a deity of sorts. I am a messenger."

"W-what is your name? Who are you? Why can I not see you?"

"I have many names. The Burning Bush. The Hand That Writes. The Watchman. The Guardian. The Sleepwalker. The Doorman. The Gatekeeper. But none of these are my secret name. I cannot tell you my real name. It is not for you to know. Names have power. Your people call me Huitzilopochtli. You may call me that as well, if you like."

Gasping, Chalco dropped the knife and fell to his knees. A sharp stone cut into his flesh, but he did not cry out. Instead, he bit his lip, lowered his eyes, and begged forgiveness. Huitzilopochtli, the guardian spirit of his people, the messenger of the gods, the Hummingbird Wizard, second only to Great Quetzalcoatl himself!

It was Huitzilopochtli who had guided the Tenochas before they settled in Oaxaca. Back then, they'd been nothing more than a wandering tribe of mongrels, the cast-offs and misfits of all the other regional tribes. They roamed the wilderness, lurking at the edges of other civilizations until they were chased away. They were a demoralized, decadent people. Then Huitzilopochtli appeared and blessed them with advice and wisdom. He told them to continue wandering. They were to be fierce but cautious, avoiding combat whenever possible, but not shrinking from their enemies either. He told them to send scouts ahead. The pioneers planted maize along the way. When the harvest was ready, they settled that area and then sent more pioneers ahead to the next location. As they traveled, Huitzilopochtli admonished them to keep him with them at all times, carrying him before them like a banner. Sacrifices were to be made in his honor, as he was a messenger for the gods and deserved tribute. The priests fed him on still-beating human hearts.

The Tenochas complied with all of his demands, and within a few generations, they ruled over all of Oaxaca, vanquishing the other tribes in the region. No longer demoralized, they were lords of the world.

Sadly, as time passed, the priests forgot about Huitzilopochtli. After all, he was merely a messenger of the gods, rather than one of the gods himself. Instead, they worshipped Quetzalcoatl and the rest of their pantheon. Chalco's generation was unsure what Huitzilopochtli even looked like. Chalco had always assumed that he was a hummingbird of some kind. He did so now, as well, and glanced up at the sky, looking for birds, but the sky was empty.

"You must turn your eyes to the ground."

"But where, lord? I do not see—"

"Here. On the agave."

Chalco crept closer to the plant. There, on one of the fronds, was a tiny, segmented worm no longer than his thumb and thinner than his arrow shafts. It had a black head and a pale, white body. Two pinprick eyes stared up at him.

"Oh…" Chalco whispered.

The worm winked.

Chalco's hands went numb. His ears rang. He thought that he might pass out.

"You… you're a worm."

"I am many things. And yes, right now I am a worm. Though it is not how I prefer to look. I have taken the form of an agave worm because I am in hiding and because the agave is linked to what must transpire today. Behemoth and his kind would find the irony amusing."

"Who?"

"Never mind. Your people don't have a name for Behemoth in your pantheon. He is one of the Thirteen, those who are neither gods nor demons and yet are mistaken for both by humanity. You worship them without understanding what they are. They, along with the Creator, are all that is left of the universe before this one. Behemoth takes the form of a Great Worm."

"Please," Chalco whispered. "I don't understand."

"Of course you don't. Humankind isn't meant to understand, for that knowledge has been denied you. Indeed, the Creator denied you knowledge of many things. Some of it is for your own good. The rest…well, I think it was terribly unfair, what happened in the Garden."

"We have gardens in Monte Alban."

"Yes, you do indeed. But those are not the Garden I speak of. Never mind. Again, it's not from your pantheon, and yet, it affects your people just the same. You should know about it. After all, Quetzalcoatl, the Plumed Serpent, is part of your belief structure, as he is to all other peoples, as well. Why not the Garden?"

"Quetzalcoatl…" Chalco's eyes grew wide. "Great Huitzilopochtli, I am sorry that I did not recognize you. I will give you the heart from my breast if it eases the insult. But before I do, I must know—are you here to herald Quetzalcoatl's return? The priests say that this is the time."

"Arise, young Chalco. Yes, it has been many years since your people have paid me tribute, but I do not require your heart. There will be time for that later. Indeed, if your people are not saved, there will be no further sacrifices to anyone."

Chalco stumbled to his feet. "Then it is true! Quetzalcoatl is about to uphold his covenant? He's returning to save us all? You have come to deliver the message."

"No, I'm afraid not. Quetzalcoatl will not return, at least, not in that form. Every time he does, you people nail him to a cross or burn him at the stake or shoot him in the chest or… well, that hasn't happened yet. It happens later. But you see what I mean? No matter what form or name he takes—Quetzalcoatl, Jesus of Nazareth, Adonis, Mohammad, Buddha, Divimoss, Kurt Cobain, Prosper Johnson, Benj—"

"I have never heard of these gods."

"Do not interrupt me again."

"I beg your forgiveness, lord."

"You have not heard of them," the worm said, "and yet you have, for they are all one and the same. They are but different incarnations of the same being."

Chalco waited until he was sure the worm was done speaking. "So Quetzalcoatl has different names?"

"Correct. So do many others. Tonatiuh, the sun god, is known as Ra to the Egyptians, and although you both believe him to have different responsibilities and worship him in different ways, he remains the same deity. Your rain god, Tlaloc, is called Cthulhu, Leviathan, Dagon, and many other things by different peoples. Huehueteotl is called Api by the Sumerians. Your Lord of the Dead, Mictlatechuhtli, is really Ob, Lord of the Siqqusim. Those last three aren't even gods, not in the true sense. They are also of the Thirteen. But regardless of their origins, be they god or devil, of this plane or another, to know their real names gives you power over them. Thus, that knowledge has also been denied you and will be until science replaces magic and you lose the ability to bind them."

"And Quetzalcoatl—or whatever his true name is—will not save us? He will not return to vanquish our enemies?"

"No."

"But he promised. The priests have said so. He promised to return."

"He has made that promise repeatedly throughout history. On this world and others. But it will not happen. It never does."

Chalco's heart sank. "Then it is true. This is indeed the end of the world."

"Not necessarily. Quetzalcoatl will not save your people. *You* will."

"M-me?"

"Indeed. That is why I am here, Chalco. Things are dire. Hernan Cortes's conquest is destroying your land. He does not serve your king. He serves Charles, the King of Spain—and his God. And though all worship stems from the same Creator, you people get so caught up in names that you think you serve different gods. That is what King Charles and Cortes believe. They believe that they are doing the work of the Creator, but they are wrong. Cortes does not care about your people. He is here for new lands and new riches, and death follows with him."

Chalco shuddered.

"Let me tell you of the future," the worm continued, "and how it will be if Cortes is not stopped. He brings with him a disease called smallpox, against which your people have no defense. This disease will race to Tenochtitlan and decimate the capital. Many will die from it, including your father—but not before he returns to infect you all. Your brother, Quintox, will be the first to die in Monte Alban, followed by Yamesha. Soon, everyone you love will be dead."

"Please...no."

"That's just the beginning. Those who die will be the lucky ones. The invaders will enslave your people and slaughter your priests. They will melt down all of your gold and mint it into coins so that King Charles can pay off his war debt. Your homes and temples will be torn down so that the Spanish can build churches and mansions in their place. What they don't destroy will be converted. Their holy men will destroy your codex and calendars. They will burn your books. Most importantly, they will teach you only of their God, and deny you access to your own gods—even though all stem from the same source...the Creator."

"Then we are lost."

"No. This can not be allowed to occur. So, as I have in the past, I am going to aid your people. I will impart a gift. And I have chosen you, Chalco, to receive that gift. I will give you a key to unlock the doors of human perception and visit unseen worlds. You will eventually gain all of the knowledge that has been forbidden to your kind, and thus, gain understanding. You will slay Cortes before he ever arrives and lead your people to triumph."

"I do not understand, lord. Why me? I am no one important. My clansmen are nothing but farmers and hunters."

"Have your priests taught you of how I appeared to your people and guided them?"

"Yes."

"I remember it well. Your people came down from the cold mountain wastes, searching for a hospitable land to call their own. Often they starved or died from exposure to the elements. Sometimes they had to fight other tribes for passage. But when they settled on the shores of Lake Texcoco in the Valley of Anahuac and began to farm, I was there waiting. I advised them to send settlers out to find more land. One of those explorers was your direct ancestor."

Chalco felt a sudden, immense pride at this revelation.

"While searching for a good location, your ancestor encountered a Toltec tribe and became involved in their affairs. Since he was only one man, they welcomed him. Your ancestor aided the Toltecs in a war against yet another tribe. He fought well and showed great valor. He slew many and turned the battle's tide. As thanks, the Toltec chieftain offered him a boon. Your ancestor asked for one of the chieftain's daughters. She was very fair, with hair like golden flax and eyes of blue.

No one in these lands had ever seen a woman like her. It was whispered that she was of the gods. Perhaps this was true. Regardless, the Toltec chieftain granted the request, impressed as he was with your ancestor's contributions."

Nodding, Chalco picked up his knife and sheathed it.

"After the boon was fulfilled," the worm continued, "your ancestor returned to his encampment with the girl in tow. But rather than marrying her, he returned to his crops and once they were planted, he sacrificed the girl. He flayed her skin and draped it over himself so that the maize might receive a blessing. He hoped the harvest would be bountiful by the time the rest of your people arrived. When the Toltecs learned of this, they attacked your ancestor. He slew them all, just as he had slain their enemies, and then he used their blood to irrigate his crops. The maize grew strong, thus, your people grew strong. Indeed, it was the finest maize and the finest people in the land. Two hundred years later, you rule over all. Your vast empire is one of the greatest this world has ever known. But within a generation, all of that will end because of Cortes. Your people will be reduced once again to a tribe of starving mongrels. That is why I come to you. Like your ancestor, *you* will save your people."

Chalco bowed again. "I am honored, Lord. But how will I do this? I am just one, and nothing special. Will you bestow special powers upon me?"

"No. As I said, I will give you a gift and teach you to open doors. With this, you will receive knowledge, which is the greatest power of all."

"But how, lord?"

"Look inside your water skin."

Chalco did as commanded. He unsealed the beeswax and pulled off the cap. Then he sniffed the contents. His nose twitched and his eyes watered. He peered inside the skin. It was filled with a yellow-brown liquid the color of ginger root.

"What happened to the pulque?"

"This is pulque, but it has been transformed into something more powerful—the drink of the gods. This is my gift. It is called tequila. One sip and you will unlock the doors of perception. Try it."

29

Hesitant, Chalco drank from the skin. He coughed. The strange liquid tasted like wood smoke and burned his throat. His stomach lurched. Gagging, he reached in his basket and pulled out his last lime. He sucked on it to rid his mouth of the taste.

"It is bitter," the worm agreed. "But the lime should help. Salt would also cut the bite. Do you carry salt with you? It is a good thing to have."

Chalco started to reply, but found that he couldn't. His tongue felt thick and swollen, and his lips were numb. It was difficult to breathe. His throat was still on fire.

"With that taste, the knowledge of how to transform pulque into this drink is passed unto your people. It stems from the agave plant. Even now, the idea takes seed in the mind of one of your clansmen. But their salvation—indeed, your entire civilization's future—lies with you. Now, take a second sip."

Chalco closed his eyes and did as commanded. He pursed his lips. The liquid's kick was still strong, but he immediately followed it with the lime. His throat felt warm, but not fiery like before. His stomach muscles clenched.

Slowly, Chalco opened his eyes…

…and stared.

A doorway floated in the air above him, hovering just off the ground. The lime fell from his gaping mouth. Chalco reached out with one trembling hand to touch the door, but then yanked it away. "What…?"

"Behold. Through that door lies the Labyrinth, a dimensional shortcut between worlds, universes, and realities. This is how my kind travels from world to world, plane to plane, back and forth through time and space."

Chalco stumbled forward, walking in a wide circle around the door. There was nothing behind it—just more mountain. He completed the circle, and stared. "But where is it?"

The worm chuckled. "Very good, Chalco. Where indeed? The door is suspended right in front of you, is it not? And yet, it isn't. The Labyrinth is nowhere and everywhere all at once. It is the in-between—the black space amidst the stars, the backdoor of reality. What you view as a doorway, is really just an extension of the Labyrinth on this level. It is indeed an entrance—and exit—but it doesn't truly exist here. The doors

30

of the Labyrinth merely connect to various levels."

"Levels?"

"Planes of existence. Different worlds and realities."

"Why couldn't I see the door before?"

"Because your eyes were not open. Normally, the only time your kind see the Labyrinth is when their spirit has departed their body. There are some among you—a select few—who know how to open the doorways and can traverse its passageways while they are still alive. But they have sacrificed much for that knowledge. I am bestowing the ability upon you so that you may save your people."

"I feel dizzy, lord. My fingers are tingling."

"That is the drink. One does not sup as the gods do without feeling the effects. Are you ready for the final sip?"

Chalco's voice trembled. "What will happen?"

"With the third taste, you will be ready. You will go through the door and travel the Labyrinth. At the far end of the hallway is another door. You will open it, and find yourself on the beach at the time of Cortes's arrival. The doorway will remain stationary behind you. The invaders will not be able to see it. It is only for your eyes. Hide in the foliage near the surf. Have your bow at the ready. Slay Cortes as he sets foot on your soil, and then return through the Labyrinth, taking the same path you took before."

Chalco picked the lime back up again, brushed the dirt off, and sucked on the fruit while he listened.

"The death of Cortes will set into motion a chain of events on this level, culminating in your people's eventual domination of the world. But be wary, Chalco. You must not be distracted. The drink of the gods sharpens your senses, but you must also maintain your wits. Although you might be tempted to travel other passageways or step through other doors, do not. Some entrances do not have exits, and not all doorways are meant to be opened. Too much knowledge is never a good thing. Stray not from the path. When you enter, go straight to the end of the passageway. After you have killed Cortes, return the way you came. Do you understand?"

Chalco nodded. Despite the lime, his mouth felt parched. His ears rang.

31

"Say it."

"I understand, Lord."

"Good." The worm crawled to the edge of the agave. "Then partake of the third sip and throw open the doors of perception."

Chalco drained the skin, and sat it next to the agave. There was only a small bit of liquid left inside. This time, he didn't need the lime. He dropped the half-eaten fruit onto the ground and wiped his mouth with the back of his hand. The tequila coursed through his body. The air seemed to thrum with energy. The hovering doorway shimmered. Overhead, an eagle cried out. Chalco took a deep breath and cast one last glance back at the worm. Then he pushed the door open, revealing a long stone corridor. Chalco stepped inside.

There was a flash of white light. Immediately, the eagle's cries ceased. Chalco glanced behind him. The door was closed. There was no sign of the mountain, the agave, or the worm. They lay on the other side of the exit. He turned around. The corridor seemed to stretch into infinity. He couldn't see the end. It was brightly lit, but there were no candles or torches. The illumination had no source. The gray stone walls were featureless, the ceiling high. There were no windows, but both sides of the hallway were lined with hundreds of closed doors. He wondered what was behind them all. More mountaintops, perhaps? Other worlds?

Admiring the masonry, Chalco touched the wall with his fingers, and then jerked them away with a gasp. The surface was cold. There was no moisture, no condensation. No texture, either—not even a crack or pit. The icy surface felt smooth. He sucked his fingertips. They were red, as if burned.

"This is not stone. It is something else."

He didn't know how he knew that, but he did. Perhaps it was the tequila. He felt it inside him. What was it Huitzilopochtli had said? The doors to reality would be thrown open and Chalco would receive knowledge. Maybe that was how he knew that the walls weren't made of stone. But if so, then why didn't he recognize the mysterious substance? Was it beyond his human reckoning? Or had the drink's effects not yet been fully realized? It didn't matter. He was experiencing something

32

that no Tenochan had ever beheld. The Labyrinth was the path to glory.

"Oh, Quintox," he whispered. "If only you could be here with me now, brother. You would be proud indeed."

He noticed that despite the length of the hall and the ceiling's height, his voice did not echo. The sound was muted. Chalco fumbled for his knife. Clutching it in one fist, he crept down the passageway. After he'd taken thirty steps, he turned around to make sure the exit was still there. It was. The door remained shut, but visible. Heart pounding, he continued on his way. He counted the closed doors as he walked by them—twelve, then twenty-four, then sixty. The corridor was obviously longer than it looked—an optical illusion of some sort, like the mirages that appeared in the desert. His father had told him all about those. A thirsty man would see water on the horizon, but when he reached it, he'd find only sand.

Occasionally, Chalco passed other corridors, intersecting with or branching off from the main hallway. He hesitated at each one, listening, but they were as silent as the rest of the Labyrinth. They, too, seemed endless—straight lines into infinity. He wondered where they went, but did not explore them, remembering Huitzilopochtli's warning. He stared ahead. When he squinted, he thought he could see the end of the hall. Despite the passageway's deceptive length, he was gaining ground.

Chalco was filled with an immense sense of pride as he continued on. Such a boon! *He* had been chosen by the gods. Him. Chalco. The gods had selected him and nobody else—not the priests or medicine men or the seasoned, battle-scarred warriors. He had never felt more alert and aware than he did at that moment. He wondered if it was another effect of the tequila or just the atmosphere of this place in general.

He thought of Quintox again. What would his family say if they could see him now? How joyous they would be, knowing that he'd been chosen by the gods to save them. When he triumphantly returned to Monte Alban, things would be different. His father and the other men could come home. Quintox would be prouder of him than ever before. And

Yamesha—her clan would certainly approve of their marriage. The priests would honor him as they did the gods. Lord Moctezuma would call upon him, or invite him to the capital. All of Oaxaca would sing his praises and his face would be forever memorialized in stone. Perhaps a village would be named after him, or maybe even a city. Songs would recount how the gods blessed him with power and how he slew Cortes and stopped the invasion. Books would be written about his exploits. He would get his own Codex in the Great Temple. It would be grand!

Lost in thought, Chalco giggled. The sound of his own laughter startled him from the daydream. He halted. The corridor continued on uninterrupted, with no end in sight. Was that possible? Surely he had traveled forward. The end— another doorway—should be visible.

He looked back the way he'd come. The hallway stretched in that direction as well, and he could no longer see the exit. The door he'd come in through was missing. Where had it gone? Had he traveled that far in such a short time? His stomach sank, and he felt a twinge of panic. Chalco squeezed the hilt of his knife until his knuckles turned white. Had he somehow taken a wrong turn while he was daydreaming, gotten disoriented and wandered off down a side passage?

"Great Huitzilopochtli," he prayed, "hear my call. Guide me, for I am lost. I did not heed your warnings or think of my people. Instead, I thought only of myself. Pride has led me astray."

Silence. The guardian spirit was not coming. Not as a worm. Not as a Hummingbird Wizard. Not at all. Chalco had never felt so afraid or alone. Dropping to his knees, he sheathed his knife and beat the floor with his fists, moaning in frustration. Like the walls, the floor was cold. He leaned back, resting against a closed door, and considered what to do next—turn back and search for the way he'd come in, or keep moving forward, hoping that he'd come to the right doorway?

He sat there, leaning against the closed door, for a very long time before he heard the water. It was coming from the other side of the door; the steady, monotonous roar of the ocean. Chalco had heard it once before in his life, when he'd accompanied his father and uncles to a religious celebration in a seaside village on Oaxaca's western shore. He'd been very young at the time, but he'd never forgotten the sound. Sometimes when he slept, he dreamed about it.

Chalco closed his eyes, put his ear to the door, and listened. It was definitely the ocean. He heard waves crashing and seabirds cawing out. His hopes rose. Maybe this was the door to the beach after all.

Jumping to his feet, Chalco opened the door and looked out into a sea. It wasn't Oaxaca's eastern shore. He wasn't even sure it was Oaxaca. The doorway hovered on the surface of the ocean. There was no land, only water. The sun hung in the sky, reflecting off the sea. Seagulls circled, hunting for fish. Chalco shielded his eyes against the glare and watched them. He smelled salt and brine. Foam-topped waves crested against the doorframe but did not splash into the corridor, prevented from entering by some kind of barrier he couldn't see. Chalco wondered if the same invisible wall would prevent him from crossing the threshold. Experimenting, he stuck his foot through the doorway. The surf lapped at his foot. The water was cold.

Slowly, Chalco pulled his foot back into the corridor and grinned. No, this wasn't the right door. This wasn't his world, or at least the part of his world he was looking for. But wherever it was, it *was* beautiful.

And then something erupted from the water. Two long, greenish-gray tentacles, each one as thick as his waist and covered with puckering suckers, thrust towards the door, grasping for him. He glimpsed a massive, shadowed bulk just beneath the surface, and then two more tendrils burst forth.

Screaming, Chalco backed against the far wall. The tentacles pushed through the open doorway and slithered across the floor. Chalco yanked his knife free of its sheath and stabbed one of the appendages as it slid across his foot. The stone blade sank into the flesh. Hot, black ichor squirted from the wound, staining his hand and splashing across the walls and floor. On the other side of the doorway came a great splash and the tentacles retreated. Chalco barely had time to free his knife.

The monster vanished beneath the surface. Chalco slammed the door shut, and the corridor was silent once more.

Steam rose from the monster's spilled blood.

When he'd stopped trembling, Chalco cleaned his hands and blade with his loincloth. Feeling helpless and unsure of what to do next, he decided to try another door.

Perhaps he'd find the right one by chance. After all, the previous exit had opened into the ocean. Maybe the next door would lead to the beach.

He put his ear to another door and listened. This time, there were no birds or waves. Just silence. Knife in hand, Chalco opened it. Inside was a small metal room. A group of people were huddled against the walls—several men, a few women, and a young boy about the same age as Quintox. When he studied the boy, Chalco was overwhelmed with a sense of familiarity—as if he'd known him before. But that was impossible. More likely the child simply reminded him of his little brother.

Their clothes were strange. One of the people seemed to be injured. He was lying in the corner, covered in blood. His face was pale and waxy. Another man brandished a weapon of some kind. Chalco didn't know what type, but assumed it was deadly, based on the fearful reactions of the others in the room every time the object was pointed at them. None of them noticed Chalco, so he eavesdropped on their conversation.

"He's not breathing, Tommy. He hasn't been for a while. I'm sorry, but it's true. Your friend is gone. He's dead. Look at him, son."

"Shut the hell up, you old fart. Just shut the fuck up right now!"

Their speech was as odd as their garments and surroundings, but Chalco could understand it—another effect of the drink, he assumed. He was fascinated by everything in the odd metal room, but this was obviously not his destination, so he reluctantly shut the door and tried another.

The third door opened into nothingness. A black void yawned before him, filled with pinpricks of light. After a moment, Chalco realized it was the night sky, as seen from high above the Earth. He'd heard the priests talk of such things. They said that the lights in the sky at night were the eyes of the gods. The door had apparently opened into a place amidst those eyes.

Stars, he thought. *I know now that these are called stars. They are not the eyes of the gods at all. Oh, this drink—this tequila—is wonderful. I'm learning so many things. When I get back to Monte Alban, I must explain this all without being labeled a heretic.*

Awestruck, he tried to find a horizon or an end to the gulf, but its boundaries were limitless. He admired the simple beauty. Knowing now that the stars weren't eyes, but suns, made them even more impressive. In the center of the darkness was a scarlet moon, slightly bigger than the one he was used to. It was an amazing sight.

And then the moon blinked.

It drifted towards him, crossing the unimaginable distance in seconds. A second moon soared into sight. The moons *were* eyes. They had no body or face. Just two huge orbs floating in the darkness. They stared at him with penetrating glares. It felt like his soul was being examined. Chalco slammed the door and the feeling disappeared.

Once he'd recovered from his fright, he tried again. The next door opened into a subterranean cavern lit by some sort of phosphorescent lichen. The rough walls were hewn, rather than naturally formed. A pile of bones lay near the door. He couldn't tell what sort of animal they'd once belonged to. A great, smokeless forge burned in the distance.

A line of pig-faced creatures lurched past, lumbering into a nearby tunnel. They had tusks and snouts and their language consisted of squeals and grunts (but again he could understand it). Despite the deformities, the pig-things walked upright like men and carried tools and weapons with them. One of them gnawed on a human forearm, stripping the meat from the bone. Their stench was incredible. Their sound was worse.

One of them stopped suddenly and raised its snout. Thick mucous dripped from the creature's nostrils. Snuffling, it turned towards him. Chalco quickly closed the door, overcome with revulsion.

He continued on. Each door was like a window on the worlds, each scene more wondrous or terrifying than the previous.

He saw a great city with tall, silver spires and men made of shiny metal rather than flesh.

He glimpsed another city built out of pure light. He watched the dead get up and walk again, hunting the living for nourishment, tearing them apart with their hands and teeth.

He laughed at a silent clown whose face was painted white. The clown tried juggling three yellow balls, but kept dropping them.

He saw a planet overcome with darkness. Blackness poured over the landscape like a wave. The darkness itself was a living creature that devoured every being it came in contact with.

He shrank away from a roaring lizard taller than the biggest temple in Monte Alban, its mouth lined with razor-sharp teeth longer than a warrior's spear. It stood over the bloody, torn corpse another, long-necked lizard.

He spied on a young, obsidian-skinned couple as they made love in the reeds along a stream bank.

He faced a tribe of creatures that were more goat than men, gathered next to a roaring campfire. Nearby them were wicker cages stuffed with terrified human women. The goat men danced in a circle around the fire and then rutted with their female captives.

He shielded his eyes from a great ball of fire that produced a mushroom-shaped cloud.

He watched people on an island flee from an army of savage beasts.

He thrilled as an armored fighter battled with a ferocious man-serpent.

He laughed in amazement at a massive creature the size of his adobe, with long, floppy ears and a trunk for a nose. The beast trampled through a steaming jungle.

He cowered at the sight of a man-sized being with gray skin, enormous black eyes, and only a slit for a mouth. The creature seemed aware of his presence. Chalco could feel it searching his mind, as if invisible fingers were combing through his brain.

He saw a coastline overrun by huge creatures that were part-crab, part-lobster, and part-scorpion. They were controlled by a race of intelligent amphibians that walked like men.

He saw a frightful being composed of pure, crackling energy, another composed entirely of sound, and a third that existed as the physical manifestation of a collective idea.

He marveled over the eruption of a great volcano that spewed molten rock and clouds of ash into the sky.

He gasped at chariots that moved without the benefit of livestock to pull them—on the ground, in the sky, and even into that black space above the Earth.

He saw births and deaths, armies clashing on a dozen battlefields, people laughing and crying. He could not know the names for all that he saw, or understand them entirely, but he knew them all the same. With each new world, he felt his consciousness expand. There would be so much knowledge to share when he made it back home.

Finally, he found what he assumed was the right door. It opened onto a beach of white sand. The sun was shining. Vegetation waved in the breeze. Rolling waves crashed onto the shore. Far out to sea, Chalco spotted an armada of ships.

"This must be it! Huitzilopochtli be praised."

He leapt through the door and onto the beach. The sun-baked sand was hot beneath his soles. It shifted beneath him as he walked. He tasted salt in the air and heard birds calling out above him. A small crab scuttled away. Washed up seashells glittered in the surf. The heat plastered his bangs to his forehead. He flipped his hair out of the way and searched for a good place to hide, somewhere that would conceal him from the ships yet offer a good vantage point and a clear shot once Cortes came ashore. He spotted a copse of trees surrounded by dunes farther up the beach, and headed for them, walking backwards, using his bow to smooth out his footprints in the sand so that nobody would see them. He looked up once, making sure that the door was still hovering above the beach.

As he concealed himself, Chalco noticed something etched in one of the tree trunks, high off the ground, certainly out of reach of a full-grown man. They were letters or glyphs of some kind, carved deep into the wood. The edges were splintered and ragged, as if claws had been used rather than a blade. The strange symbols were in another language, but the tequila gave him understanding of what they said—if not their meaning.

CROATOAN

Was it a name? A place? A tribe of people? He didn't know,

despite the drink's influence. It sounded…unclean. Ominous.

In the distance, three small boats cast off from the larger ships. Their flags fluttered in the wind. Men sat perched in them, watching the shoreline. Kneeling in the sand, Chalco strung his bow and notched an arrow, waiting. The breeze died down and the birds grew silent. Even the ocean seemed still. And then, something snuffled behind him. Screeching, the birds took flight, fleeing the area. Still crouching, Chalco whirled around, pointing his arrow in the direction of the noise.

Several yards away, a terrible creature rose from behind a shifting dune. It was almost three times his height, and covered with white, matted fur. The thing was broad-shouldered and barrel-chested, and its powerful arms hung down to its knees. Talon-tipped fingers clenched and unclenched. The monster's face was almost human, except for a wide mouth filled with gleaming fangs, and two black, brooding eyes above a flat nose. Seeing Chalco, it snorted in surprise. Chalco was reminded of a cat. The thing's ears looked feline, pointed and twitching. A monstrous phallus swung between its legs.

Chalco's heart beat. Once. Twice.

The creature charged.

Chalco let his arrow fly.

The thing grunted as the arrow plunged into its chest. The shaft protruded from its breast, the white fur turning crimson around the wound. The monster never slowed. It snapped the shaft with one hand and lunged for him.

Biting his lip, Chalco notched another arrow and let loose. The beast snatched it from the air and tossed it aside.

Chalco leapt to his feet and ran. Behind him, he heard trees snapping as the creature gave chase. The sand shook with each loping stride the monster took. Its growls echoed across the beach.

It can't see the doorway, Chalco thought as he fled. *Only I can. If I make it back into the Labyrinth, it won't be able to follow.*

The beast closed the gap between them. Chalco heard its harsh breathing. Its stink fouled the air. Flinging his bow aside, he pounded across the sand, forcing his legs to go faster. His lungs burned. The wind howled in his ears—or maybe it was just his pursuer.

Chalco dived headfirst through the floating doorway. He landed in the corridor, banging his head on the stone that wasn't stone. The breath rushed from his lungs. He rolled across the floor, coming to rest against the wall. Rubbing his head, Chalco drew his knife.

Outside, on the beach, the growls changed to laughter.

Animals don't laugh. That thing is intelligent.

As he watched, it headed straight for the doorway.

It can't see me. It can't...

The monster plunged an enormous, fur-covered hand through the open door, grasping at him. Screaming, Chalco slashed at it with his knife. The hand withdrew, and then reached for him again. The blade bit deeper. Blood spattered the floor. Enraged, the beast pulled away again.

Chalco held his breath.

The monster slammed against the doorframe, heaving its bulk through the opening. The door seemed to shimmer and stretch to accommodate the creature's size. One hand thrust through, then an arm, then another. The entrance grew wider as the beast's head followed.

Chalco took advantage of the arduous progress to escape. He slid out of the monster's reach and sprinted down the hallway, ignoring all of the other doors. His feet pounded in silence. His breath stiffened in his throat.

Behind him, the monster raged. Then it spoke for the first time. Its cadence was slow and halting. The rough, guttural sound terrified Chalco as much as the beast itself did.

"You...not...escape...Meeble."

Chalco turned left down a side passage and kept running, not looking back. Closed doors flashed by on both sides, each one of them an invitation to more terror. Who knew what lurked behind them? Wisdom was a curse. He wanted to go home, wanted to go back to being a boy.

Wanted to forget.

He ran for a very long time, and the beast—Meeble—pursued him. Usually, it was far behind, but several times it nearly caught him. He wondered what the creature was, and what its name meant. He'd never seen anything like it before. He doubted any of his clan had, either.

41

Finally, Chalco came to a dead end. A double door, larger than the others, stood before him. He wondered what new horror waited on the other side. Behind him, around the corner, he heard the monster catching up. It snorted like a bull. Its breathing sounded like a geyser.

Closing his eyes, Chalco opened the door and stepped through. Wind brushed against his face. He opened his eyes, but it was too late.

He fell into darkness...

...and did not stop.

Back on the mountaintop, the doorway flickered and then vanished. Still perched on the agave plant and still in the form of a worm, Huitzilopochtli hung his head and cried. He had failed. Humanity was not ready for the knowledge tequila provided. Perhaps they never would be. They were too prideful, too worldly—too human.

He'd deceived his masters. Slipped away and hid inside this form, hoping to tip the scales in humanity's favor—turn the tide of infinity. But he had failed. Soon, he would be found out. He could not hide forever, not even outside the Labyrinth.

As the sun began to set, Huitzilopochtli inched his way down the agave and onto the ground. The soil was cooler now. He crawled across it. A shadow fell over him. He had time to look up and then the bird plunged toward him. Wriggling beside the agave to avoid the flashing beak, he fell into Chalco's discarded water skin, which had a few drops of tequila in the bottom. The worm struggled, and then became still.

Night descended. The wildlife returned to the mountain, and in Monte Alban, Quintox waited for Chalco to return home.

He never did.

But eventually, their father and uncles returned to Monte Alban. Death came with them. The worm's prophecy came to pass.

And the doors were closed to humanity.

And that is why to this day, some people believe in the legend of tequila. They believe that tequila is a gift of the gods. That it will grant knowledge of the universe and open the doors of perception. And they also believe that eating the worm will allow them to visit an unseen world.

But they never do.

Instead they fall.

When you write for a living, you usually write every day. And while you (hopefully) never lose that sense of magic and wonder, it is easy to become bogged down in the process. There are deadlines and publisher demands. Editors and readers are eager to suggest what you should really be writing, especially if you want to get paid. And if your mortgage payment relies on that next sale, you tend to at least consider their suggestions. If you're not careful, crafting stories can become more like work and less like fun.

So it's always a treat when you get to try something different and explore new literary horizons. Just like in a relationship, experimentation can reinvigorate a writer's muse.

That's what this story was to me. An experiment—and great fun, as well. After reading Jack Ketchum's masterful fable, The Transformed Mouse, *I fell in love with fables all over again and wondered if there were any new ones to tell. Luckily, I was thinking about this while drinking a bottle of tequila.*

Tequila has no concrete history. There are a number of different theories as to how it came to be. If you don't believe me, check the internet. Tequila and mezcal experts argue over the drink's origins, what actually constitutes the drink, where the worm came from, etc. As an enthusiast, this seems like a shame to me. And since nobody can apparently agree on its true origin, I figured I'd make one up.

Thus, I wrote a fable detailing how the "drink of the gods" came to be, incorporating much of its trappings and mystique. It's fiction, of course. Historians might point out things I got wrong. I suggest they have a shot and shut the fuck up. It's my mythos and I can do what I want with it.

Indeed...my mythos—the ongoing Labyrinth saga, about which much was revealed here. The second half of this story is certainly not for the uninitiated. It is decidedly mythos heavy. There are references to various novels and stories, characters and villains. If you are indeed new to my works, then an explanation is probably in order. The Labyrinth is a dimensional shortcut between worlds, universes, and realities, and is only accessible to those who know how to open the doors. Glimpses of this mythos wind through everything I've ever written. Every novel, every novella, and every short story contains a hint of it. Yet, I've purposely tried to keep those links vague, so that new readers can also enjoy the stories and books. You shouldn't have to read Terminal *to understand* Ghoul, *or* The Rising *to enjoy* Kill Whitey. *And yet, for the hardcore fans, the folks who read everything I write, the mythos is there—and they love it. Indeed, they want more, as evidenced by the preponderance of threads on my message board and Facebook and Twitter in which people ask for more.*

This was my gift to them. It's a love letter to one of my favorite vices (tequila) and a thank you to some of my favorite people (my readers). I hope that you enjoyed it. This novella was first published as a beautiful limited edition hardcover by Bloodletting Press. It also appeared in my short story collection Unhappy Endings, *which is now out-of-print.*

BURYING

BETSY

We buried Betsy on Saturday. We dug her up on Monday and let her come inside, but then on Wednesday, Daddy said we had to put her back in the ground again.

Before that, we'd only buried her about once a month. Betsy got upset when she found out she had to go back down so soon. She wanted to know why. Daddy said it was more dangerous now. Only way she'd be safe was to hide her down there below the dirt, where no one could get to her without a lot of trouble. Betsy cried a little when she climbed back into the box, but Daddy told her it would be okay. I cried a little, too, but didn't let no one else see me do it.

We gathered around the spot in the woods; me, Daddy, Betsy, and my older brother Billy. Betsy is six, I'm nine, and Billy is eleven. Betsy, Billy and Benny—that's what Mom had named us. Daddy said she liked names that began with the letter 'B'.

Betsy's eyes were big and round as she lay down inside the wooden box. She clutched her water bottle and the little bag of cookies that Daddy had given her. The other hand held her stuffed bear. He was missing one eye and the seams had split on his head. He didn't have a name.

We closed the lid, and Betsy whimpered inside the box.

"Please, Daddy," she begged. "Can't I just stay up this once?"

"We've been over this. It's the only way to keep you safe. You know what could happen otherwise."

"But it's dark and it's cold, and when I go potty, it makes a mess."

Daddy shivered.

"Maybe we could let her stay up just this once," Billy said. "Me and Benny can keep an eye on her."

Daddy frowned. "You want your little sister to end up like the others? You know what can happen."

Billy nodded, staring at the ground. I didn't say anything. I probably couldn't have anyway. There was a lump in my throat, and it grew as Betsy sobbed inside the box.

We sealed her up tight, and hammered the lid back on with some eight-penny nails. There was a small round hole in the lid. We fed a garden hose through the opening, so Betsy could breathe. Then Daddy got his caulk gun out of the shed and sealed the little crack between the hose and the lid, so that no dirt would fall down into the box. Finally, we each grabbed a rope and lowered the box down into the hole.

"Careful," Daddy grunted. "Don't jostle her."

We shoveled the dirt back down on her. The hole was about eight feet deep, and even with the three of us it took a good forty minutes. Her cries got quieter as we filled the hole. Soon enough, we couldn't hear her at all. We laid the big squares of sod over the fresh grave and tamped them down real good. Made sure the hose was sticking out at an angle, so rainwater wouldn't rush inside it. When we were done, Daddy gathered some fallen branches and leaves and scattered them around. Then he stepped back, wiped the sweat from his forehead with his t-shirt, and nodded with approval.

"Looks good," he said. "Somebody comes by, there's no way they could tell she's down there."

He was right. Only thing that seemed odd was that piece of green garden hose, and even that kind of blended with the leaves. It looked just like a scrap, tossed aside and left to rot.

"And," Daddy continued, "it will take a long time to dig her back up. It would wear anybody out."

We walked back up to the house and got washed up for dinner. I had blisters on my hands from all the shoveling, and there was black dirt under my fingernails. It took a long time to get my hands clean, but I felt better once they were. Daddy and Billy were already sitting at the table when I came downstairs. I pulled out my seat. Betsy's empty chair made me sad all over again.

Dinner was cornbread and beans. Daddy fixed them on the stove. They were okay, but not nearly as good as Mom's used to be. Daddy's cornbread crumbled too much, especially when you tried to spread butter on it. And his beans tasted kind of plain. Mom's had been much better.

Mom had been gone a little over a year now. Didn't seem that long some days, but then on others, it seemed like forever. Sometimes, I couldn't remember what she looked like anymore. I'd get the picture album down from the hutch and stare at her photos to remind me how her face had been. And her eyes. Her smile. I hated that I couldn't remember.

But I still remembered how her cornbread tasted. It was fine.

I missed her. We all did, especially Daddy, more and more these days.

After dinner, Billy and me washed the dishes while Daddy went outside to smoke. When he came back in, we watched the news. Daddy let us watch whatever we wanted to at night, up until our bedtime, but we always had to watch the news first. He said it was important that we knew about the world, and how things really were, especially since we didn't go to school.

Just like every night, the news was more of the same; terrorism, wars, bombings, shootings, people in Washington hollering at each other—and the pedophiles. Always the pedophiles... A teenaged girl had been abducted behind a car wash in Chicago. Another was found dead and naked alongside the riverbank in Ashland, Kentucky. Two little boys were missing in Idaho, and the police said the suspect had a previous record. And our town was mentioned, too. The news lady talked about the twelve little girls who'd gone missing in the last year, and how they'd all been found dead and molested.

Molested... it was a scary word.

Daddy said it was all part of the world we lived in now. Things weren't like when he'd been a kid. There were pedophiles everywhere these days. They'd follow you home from school, get you at the church, or crawl through your bedroom window at night. They'd talk to you on the internet— trick you into thinking they were someone else, and then meet up with you. That's why Daddy said none of us were allowed on the computer, and why he didn't let us go to school. Child molesters could be anyone—teachers, priests, doctors, policemen, even parents.

Daddy said it was an urge, a sickness in their brain that made them do those things. He said even if they went to jail or saw a doctor, there weren't no cure. When the urge was on them, there was no helping it. Unless they learned to control it, and even then, there weren't no guarantees.

I went to bed but couldn't sleep. I lay there in the darkness and listened to Billy snoring beneath me. We had bunk beds, and it was a familiar sound—sort of comforting. One of those noises that you hear every night, the ones that tell you everything is okay—your big brother snoring, your little sister in the room across the hall, your Daddy's footsteps as he tiptoes down the hall in the middle of the night.

But tonight, there was just Billy. Daddy wouldn't be tiptoeing down the hall. He'd left just as soon as we went to bed. I heard the car pull out of the driveway. He was gone, out to fulfill his urges. He'd told me and Billy that he'd always had them, but he'd been able to control them until Mom died. After she was gone, they'd gotten stronger. He knew the urges were wrong, but he had to do what he had to do.

It's almost midnight now, and I still can't sleep. Daddy's not back yet.

Tomorrow, another little girl will be missing.

But at least it won't be Betsy.

Betsy is buried in the ground, safe from Daddy's urges.

The idea for this story took root during a conversation with my then-second wife. We were discussing how, when I was a kid, my parents let me ride my bike all over town and stay gone all day, coming home only for dinner. Back then, they didn't worry about some nut abducting me. It saddens me that things have changed. I want our son to enjoy the same freedoms I had as a boy, but I also want to protect him from the bad people out there. "Burying Betsy" grew out of that. At first, the father was just burying his daughter to keep her safe, but halfway through the first draft, the twist suggested itself to me and the story became something quite different from its original premise.

This story previously appeared in Cemetery Dance *magazine, and was re-printed in my short story collections* Fear of Gravity *and* A Little Silver Book of Streetwise Stories, *both of which are long out-of-print. It was also adapted for a graphic novel.*

DUST

Two months later...

She still jumped every time she heard an airplane.
The sound never left her. In her sleep, at lunch, in the shower, watching TV—Laura relived it over and over again.
Emerging from the subway into the warm September day. Thunder crackles overhead; a stuttering, staccato sound. White noise. The thunder is loud (so loud—everything in the city is loud but this drowns it all out) and she stares upward in startled amazement (but not fear—not yet). The thunder is a plane, roaring toward the towers. Then the sky is falling and there is fire and now comes the fear because that is where Dallas is working.
The panic and chaos that ensued after the second plane were distant events; detached from reality. Only that first sound, the sound of the plane overhead, was real.
She'd been on her way home from the night shift. On a normal day, Dallas would have just been getting up. Laura would have arrived at the twelfth floor apartment they shared, and she'd tell him all about her night while he shaved and dressed for work. They'd discuss their plans for the weekend, when neither had to work. They did this every day. On a normal day.
But none of these things happened because Dallas left her a voice mail on her cell phone. He was going in early, anticipating a telecom rally when the market opened. Grubman said it was going to be big, and you could trust Grubman. Grubman knew his shit.
Dallas went to work early. He crossed the street. Bought a cup of coffee and the *Post*. Got on the elevator and scanned the headlines on the way up. Adjusted his tie. Walked into the office. Sat at his desk.
And never came home.
Neither had Laura; not since it happened. She never arrived home because of the sound, that terrible jet engine sound. The bottom fell out of her world that day and the center did not hold, did not pass go, did not collect two hundred dollars.
She'd spent the first few nights with some friends in Brooklyn, before moving to her sister's house in Jersey. She

53

couldn't go home, they told her. The area was unsafe. They had to determine if the structure was sound.

Dallas had no funeral because there was nothing to bury. She waited. Eventually, she returned to work. She waited. Then she waited some more.

Finally, the call came. They told her she could go back to get her valuables. There was still a lot of work to be done; windows to be replaced, apartments to be cleaned. Cosmetic work, the lady on the phone had said. But she could collect her things at least, and hopefully move back in within a month.

Now here she was, back at the place where they'd lived—a place she no longer recognized. Her neighborhood was a monument to sorrow. Its geography was forever altered.

The first thing she noticed (after the wreckage) was the birds. Like any other place, the concrete and steel canyons of the city had their own form of wildlife. Squirrels and rats. Dogs and cats. Flies and pigeons. These were common.

But turkey buzzards were something new.

Laura watched one soar overhead; its black, mottled wings outstretched to catch the breeze. The bird reminded her of the plane. Her breath caught in her throat. The frigid November air encircled her, and she was afraid. The shopping bag in her hands grew heavy, and its contents sloshed around inside.

The buzzard joined the other scavenger birds, circling the devastation from above. She wondered if it was the smell that attracted them, or some deeper instinct. Perhaps they waited on the promise of more to come?

She edged her way around the site, shifting the weight of the bulky, misshapen shopping bag from arm to arm. Workers called to each other from across the rubble. Heavy machinery roared to the accompaniment of jackhammers and the white-hot hiss of acetylene torches. Somewhere beyond it all, where the city still lived, came the echoes of traffic; the comforting, familiar chaos of horns and sirens. The sounds were muted, though. The mood here in the dead zone was palpable, and for a moment, Laura was convinced that the circling buzzards didn't ride the wind currents, but instead, floated aloft on the waves of despair rising from the wreckage.

She continued on to her building, and found something

worse than the carnage. Something worse than the circling scavengers or the noisy silence or the twisted girders or the smell coming from the ruins.

Dust. The sidewalks and the building itself were caked with dust. Her feet left tracks in it as she slowly climbed the steps. It coated her palm when she pulled the door open. The haggard security guard in the lobby was covered in it. Dust floated around him like a halo as he solemnly studied her letter of permission. He had her sign a dusty piece of paper on a dusty clipboard.

It's the towers, she thought, *and everything that was inside them. It's dead people.*

She felt a moment of panic as the doors closed behind her and the elevator lurched upward. She set the bag down on the floor, grateful for a moment's respite. The soft whir of the motor and the cables sounded like the plane.

The dust was even here, inside the elevator. She brushed at the control panel with her fingertips and they came away white and powdery.

Dead people.

With each step, I'm breathing in dead people. I'm breathing in Dallas.

The elevator halted, and Laura froze for a moment, unable to go on. The bell rang impatiently, and she picked up the bag, grunting with the effort. She took one faltering step forward, then another. The doors hissed shut behind her.

The dust was much worse here on her floor. The hallway was covered in it, and the beautiful red carpet was now buried beneath gray ash. It clung to the paintings on the wall and coated the mirrors.

The hallway was quiet. Laura started forward. She heard a hoarse coughing echoing from behind her neighbor's door. Laura stopped and listened. The coughing came again, harsh and ragged, followed by the sounds of movement.

Timidly, she knocked. There was a moment's pause and then the door opened.

"Laura! Oh darling, it's so good to see you." An elderly German lady waddled out and squeezed Laura tight.

"Hello, Doris," Laura sat the bag down and hugged her

back. "I'd been worried about you. How's Jack?"

"He's still in the hospital. Cranky as ever. They're doing another skin graft tomorrow. And his mind... It's... How are you, dear?"

"I'm—" and then she couldn't finish because the lump in her throat made speech impossible. Then the tears came, carving tracks through the dust on her face.

Doris held her tight and cooed softly in her ear, swaying them back and forth.

"I'm sorry," Laura finally apologized, wiping her eyes. "I miss Dallas. It's just too much."

"I know, dear. I know. Do you want me to go in with you?"

Laura shook her head. "No. Thank you Doris, but I think I need to do this by myself. You understand?"

"Of course, Laura. You go on and do what need's doing. I'll be here for awhile. I'm just sorting through the mess. The windows inside our apartment are broken, and this damned dust is everywhere! They were supposed to put plywood up until they got them repaired, but they haven't yet. Too many other things going on, I guess."

Doris coughed again.

Laura squeezed her hand tightly, and then picked her bag up and moved on.

She came to her apartment door and paused. Something was moving on the other side. She put her ear to the door and she heard it again; a light, rustling sound.

Dallas? Was he alive all this time, and waiting for her? Maybe he had amnesia, like in a movie, and this was the only place he remembered.

She put her key in the lock, turned it, and opened the door. The breeze smacked her face. Something fluttered in the shadows. Laura fumbled in the darkness, found the switch, and flicked it, flooding the apartment with light.

A pigeon cooed at her from the windowsill, annoyed at the disturbance. Then it flew away through the broken window. It hadn't been Dallas. It was just a bird. Laura felt foolish and sad and angry. It hadn't been Dallas because Dallas was gone. He'd left for work early because Grubman had said there would be a telecom rally and now he was dead and Grubman was dead and everybody else was dead, too. Dallas was gone and there wasn't even anything to bury because he was dust. Just dust in the wind, like the song.

The apartment was buried beneath it. Piles and drifts of gray ash covered the furniture and the floor, and dust motes floated in the rays of the dim bulb in the ceiling. It swirled in and out of the broken windows, and out the open door behind her into the hallway.

She shut the door and sat her bag down next to the coat rack. The can inside the bag clanked against the tile, and the liquid sloshed again.

Dallas stared back at her from the wall, frozen in time behind the glass frame. Their trip to Alcatraz, when they'd visited Gene and Kay in San Francisco last year. Dallas was laughing at the camera with that smile. It was his smile that she'd fallen in love with first.

In the kitchen, something caught her attention. A yellow post-it note, stuck to the dirty fridge, with her name scrawled on it in his handwriting.

Laura,

I had to go in early. Grubman was on CNBC this morning, and he's saying that Worldcom and Quest will bounce back today. Tried calling your cell but I got your voice mail. My turn to cook dinner tonight. How's fish sound? Hope you had a good night at work! Love ya!

Dallas

Laura sobbed. She reached out to touch the note, and her fingers came away gritty. It, too, was covered in dust.

"I miss you baby. I miss you so bad."

The wind howled through the broken glass, kicking up mini-dust clouds all throughout the apartment. The dust swirled toward her, encircling her ankles. Laura turned, and for just a moment, she heard his voice in the wind. The dust hung suspended before her, twirling in mid-air, and she saw his face within the cloud. Dallas smiled at her, and even though it was gray and powdery, it was still his smile. The one she had fallen in love with. More of the cloud took shape now; shoulders, arms, his chest. Each muscle was chiseled perfectly from the dust.

"I want to hold you, Dallas."

She reached for him and her fingers passed through his center. As suddenly as it had begun, the winds stopped and the ashes dissipated, floating to the floor. Laura pulled her hand away. The center of the dust cloud was cold, and the tips of her fingers turned pale. It reminded her of when she'd been a little girl, and built a snowman without wearing her gloves.

"Dallas?"

There was no answer. She knelt to the floor and scooped the ash in her hands, letting it sift through her fingers. Another gust of wind blew through the room, gently carrying the dust away.

"I miss you."

She went back out into the hall and knocked on Doris' door.

"All set dear?"

"If it's okay with you, Doris, I think I'm going to hang around awhile."

"I understand, Laura. Take what time you need. It's important to do so. I'll be off for the hospital then. Jack will be grumbling if I don't get back soon."

"Give him my best?"

"I surely will. And you must come see him soon, yes?"

Laura nodded, unable to speak.

She went back to her apartment and shut the door, waiting for the sounds of the old lady's departure. When she was sure Doris had gone, she rummaged inside her shopping bag and pulled out the gas can and the pills. She swallowed the pills first, and waited for them to kick in. Then, as she grew drowsy, Laura unscrewed the lid and splashed gasoline all over the floor, the walls, and the furniture. It carved little rivulets in the dust, and the smell of it wasn't at all unpleasant. It was welcome. The odor blocked out the stench coming from the pit below.

She was getting sleepy.

Laura lit the match.

"Dallas."

The wind answered her with a sigh, and the dust began to move again, caressing her arms and face.

She was asleep before the flames touched her.

The fireman wiped a grimy hand across his brow. "Christ, like we needed this on top of everything else?"

"Least the building wasn't re-occupied yet," his partner said. "And the fire was contained to just a few apartments."

"Wasn't re-occupied my ass! What do you call those? Squatters?" He pointed at the two mounds of dust on the floor. They were both human shaped, lying together side-by-side. He let his eyes linger on them a moment longer, and swore that the dust piles were holding hands.

The other man shrugged. "Optical illusion? A joke? Fuck, do you know how hot it had to be in here to reduce a human body to ash like that? Couldn't have happened, man, or else this entire building would be toast."

"So what the fuck are they?"

"Just one of those weird things, like the photos you see in *The Fortean Times*. Simulacra they call it, or something like that. The security guard said there were only a few tenants that had come back to get their stuff, and he was pretty sure they were gone."

"Well, it still gives me the creeps. Let's go."

After they left, the dust began to swirl again. Sheets of heavy plywood had finally been put into place, sealing up the burned apartment, but the air moved. A wind blew through the room. It came not from the windows or from the hall, but from somewhere else.

The mounds of ash rose and embraced. Then, still holding hands, they fell apart; floating away until there was nothing left.

This story appeared in my second short-story collection, Fear of Gravity, *and was reprinted in* A Little Silver Book of Streetwise Stories *and as a promotional chapbook (along with a story by author Kelli Owen). All three are out-of-print.*

"Dust" bounced around in my head for a year before I wrote it. One month after the 9/11 attacks, I went to New York City to do a live appearance at the Housing Works Bookstore. As I was walking down the street, I happened to glance up and spotted a turkey buzzard flying between the buildings. Then another. And another. Turkey buzzards are a common sight in rural areas like the town I grew up in. Any time there's a dead animal in the field or on the road, you'll find them circling. But I'd never seen one in the city. Especially New York City. A newspaper vendor told me the birds were going to Ground Zero—the wreckage of the World Trade Center. In some ways, that image of the scavenger birds, and the newspaper vendor's explanation for their presence, chill me more than the footage of the planes hitting the towers or the Pentagon ever can. A year after, in October of 2002, I tired to write it out of my system. "Dust" was the result.

FADE TO
NULL

She woke to the sound of thunder, lying in a strange bed with no memory of who she was or where she was, and panic nearly overwhelmed her. Her stomach clenched. Her breaths came in short gasps. Frantic, she glanced around the room for clues, but familiarity eluded her. The room was small, equipped with a dresser, a writing desk, and a chair with one leg shorter than the others. Atop the dresser sat a slender blue-glass vase with some flowers in it.

The flowers soothed her, but she didn't know why.

She studied the rest of the room. Looming overhead were the cracked, yellowing panels of a drop ceiling. The carpet was light green, the wallpaper pastel. Framed prints hung on the wall—Monet, Kincaid, Rockwell. She wondered how it was possible that she knew their names but didn't know her own. The closet door was slightly open, revealing a stranger's clothes. There was only one window, and the blinds were closed tight. If the room had a door, other than the closet, she couldn't see it.

The sheets were thin and starchy, and rubbed against her skin like sandpaper. They felt damp from sweat. Clenching the sheets in both fists, she raised them slightly and peered beneath. She was dressed in a faded sleeping gown with a dried brown stain over one breast. What was it? Gravy? Mud? Blood? Except for her underwear, she was bare beneath the gown.

She considered calling for help, but decided against it. She was afraid—afraid of who, or what, might answer her summons. Despite the fact that the room seemed empty, she couldn't help but feel like there was someone else in here with her. Someone *unseen.*

The thunder boomed again. Blue-white light flashed from behind the closed blinds, and for a moment, she saw glimpses of other people in the room with her—a man, a woman, and a little girl. They were like the images on photo negatives, stark against the room's feeble light, but at the same time, flickering and ghostly—composed of television static. The man stood by her bedside, dressed in a white doctor's coat. A stethoscope dangled around his neck. He held a clipboard. The woman stood next to him, wearing a simple but pretty blouse. She seemed tired and sad. The little girl sat in the wobbly chair, rocking back and forth on the crooked legs.

"It's okay, Mika. Grandma is just having a bad dream."
The voice was distant. Muted. An echo. And female.
She tried to scream, but only managed a rasping, wheezy sigh.
The three figures vanished with the next blast of thunder, blinking out of existence as if they'd never been there at all.
Maybe they hadn't.
She was dimly aware that she had to pee.
When the drum roll of thunder sounded again, the drop-ceiling disappeared as quickly as the ghost-people had. Everything else in the room remained the same—the drab furnishings, the dim light—but in the ceiling's place was a purple, wounded sky. Boiling clouds raced across it, but she felt no wind. Although the temperature hadn't changed, she shivered. The pressure on her bladder increased. She relaxed, and felt a sudden rush of warmth. Then the violet sky split open, revealing a black hole, and it began to rain desiccated flowers.
'Flowers,' she thought. 'There are flowers on the dresser. Ellen brought them.'
Then she wondered who Ellen was.
Dried petals continued to shower the bed, tickling her nose and cheeks. She sighed. The feeling was not unpleasant. Then, as quickly as it had begun, the rain of flower petals stopped—replaced by something else. Her eyes widened in terror. A squadron of bulbous flies poured from the hole in the sky, buzzing in a multitude of languages. Their bodies were black, their heads green like emeralds. They circled the room in a swirling pattern. A flock of birds plunged out of the hole, giving chase. The thunder increased, inside the room with her now. The noise was deafening. The flies scattered and the birds squawked in fright. A black, oily feather floated gently towards her.
She tried to sit up, but her fatigue weighed her like a stone. All she could do was lie there and watch. Listen. Wonder.
Where was she? What was this? What was happening?
She thought again of the flowers. They'd been brought by... who, exactly? She couldn't remember. Someone. She thought it might be important.

The warmth dissipated. She was cold again. Her fear was replaced by a powerful sense of frustration in both her physical discomfort and her confusion. Why couldn't she remember anything?

Above her, the sky continued to weep. Now, strands of DNA fell in ribbons, forming puddles on the bed and floor. Life stirred within those puddles, writhing and squirming. The thunder changed into a voice—a deity, perhaps, screaming. It was a terrible sound. She clasped her hands over her ears and tried to block it out. She'd heard screams like this before. Perhaps she'd even made them, at one time. They sounded like the symphony of birthing pains.

A large puddle of liquid tissue had formed on the sheet in front of her, right between her legs. As she watched, something wriggled from the puddle—a one-inch tentacle, about the thickness of a pencil. There was an eyeball attached to one end of the tendril. It stared at her, and as she watched, the pupil dilated.

In the background, the deity was still screaming. She no longer cared. Her attention was focused on the tentacle-thing. The creature groped feebly at her gown, and then pulled itself forward. She slapped her hand down on it, pressing it into the mattress and grinding her palm back and forth. The tentacle squeaked—even though it lacked a mouth—and then lay still. She removed her hand. All that remained of the thing was a pinkish-white blob of mucus. Slime dripped from her hand.

Silence returned. The disembodied screaming stopped. So did the thunder. The flies and the birds turned to vapor. The hole in the sky closed up, and second later, the drop ceiling reappeared.

"Please," she whispered. "Please... please..."

Then, new voices spoke. A man and a woman.

"She used to love to paint. I thought bringing some of this might help, but she can't even hold the paintbrush."

"Yes. Her motor skills are decreasing rapidly."

"How long does she have?"

"In this stage of Alzheimer's, it is difficult to say. I've seen some hang on for years after the fourth stage has set in. Others go quickly. All we can do is keep her comfortable."

"I just hate bringing Mika to see her like this, you know? I'm worried about how it will effect her."

"That's understandable, Ellen. And while some studies suggest that it's beneficial for patients, we can't even really be sure that your mother is aware of the presence of those around her. I know it's not much comfort, but at least she's calm and peaceful, for the most part."

"Who are you?" she moaned. "Where are you?"

She closed her eyes and let her cheek loll against the pillow, wishing the sky would rain flowers again.

"Who am I?" she whispered. "Please..."

The voices disappeared.

At last, she slept.

When she awoke again, the room was dark and cold. She shivered. There were flowers on the dresser, but she no longer knew what they were.

This story started as nothing more than a fragment. About one-hundred words of it was originally written for one of those multi-author collaboration projects—two dozen authors each contributing to one short story. Unfortunately, the project never came to fruition. I no longer remember who was involved or what the premise was. All I know is that it was never published (if it had been, I'm sure I'd have a contract or a copy of the book around here somewhere).

Anyway, I bought a new computer and I was in the process of transferring my files over to it when I ran across this old, forgotten fragment. I re-worked it into this story. Alzheimer's has impacted my family in a very personal way. It's a truly terrifying disease. I find it especially scary because none of us really know what's going on inside the mind of the victim.

"Fade To Null" has only appeared once before—in my now out-of-print short story collection Unhappy Endings.

BUNNIES IN AUGUST

One year later…

He shouldn't have come here. Not today. Especially not today.

This is where it happened, he thought. *This is where Jack died.*

Gary stood beneath the water tower. It perched atop the tallest hill in town, right between the Methodist church cemetery, and the rear of the tiny, decrepit strip mall (abandoned when Wal-Mart moved in two miles away), and a corn field. The tower was a massive, looming, blue thing, providing water to the populace below. Every time he saw it, (which was all the time, because it was visible from everywhere in town) Gary was reminded of the Martian tripods from *War of the Worlds.* When Jack was old enough to read the graphic novel adaptation, it had reminded him of the same thing.

"It looks like one of the Martian robots, doesn't it Daddy? Doesn't it? Let's pretend the Martians are invading!"

The first tear welled up. Then another. They built to a crescendo. Surrendering, Gary closed his eyes and wept. A warm summer breeze rustled the treetops above him. His breath caught in his throat. He tried to swallow the lump, and found he couldn't. Sweat beaded his forehead. The heat was stifling. His skin prickled, as if on fire. As if he was burning. The wind brushed against him like caressing flames.

Blinking the tears away, he glanced back up at the water tower and wondered how he could bring it down. He saw it every day—on the drive home, from the grocery store parking lot, the backyard, even his bedroom window—and each time he was reminded of his son. The tower's presence was inescapable. How to erase its existence—and thus, the memories? A chainsaw was out of the question. The supports were made of steel. Explosives maybe? Yeah. Sure. He was a fucking insurance salesman. Where was he going to find explosives?

He hated the water tower. It stood here as an unwanted reminder, a dark monument to Jack.

This was where it happened.

This used to be their playground.

Weekends had always been their time together. During the week, Gary and Susan both worked, he at the insurance office and she from home, typing up tape-recorded court transcripts. Jack had school, fourth grade, where he excelled in English and Social Studies, but struggled with Math and Science. Gary didn't see them much on weeknights, either. He'd had other… obligations.

Leila's face popped into his mind, unbidden. He pushed her away.

Get thee behind me, Satan.

The weekends were magic. Once he'd waded through the mind-numbing tedium of domestic chores; grocery shopping, mowing the lawn, cleaning the gutters, and anything else Susan thought up for him to do while she sat at home all day long; after all that, there was Daddy and Jack time. Father and son time. Quality time.

Jack's first word had been 'Da-da'.

Gary had loved his son. Loved him so much that it hurt, sometimes. Despite how clichéd it may have sounded to some people, the pain was real. And good. When Jack was little, Gary used to stand over his crib and watch him sleeping. In those moments, Gary's breath hitched up in his chest—a powerful, overwhelming emotional wave. He'd loved Susan like that too, once upon a time, when they'd first been married. Before job-related stress and mortgage payments and their mutual weight gain—and before Susan's little personality quirks, things he'd thought were cute and endearing when he'd first met her, the very things he'd fallen in love with after the initial physical attraction, became annoying rather than charming. They knew everything there was to know about each other, and thus, they knew too much. Boredom set in, and worse, a simmering complacency that hollowed him out inside and left him empty. When Jack came along in their fifth year of marriage, Gary fell in love all over again, and his son had filled that hole.

At least temporarily…

Parental love was one thing. That completed a part of him. But Gary still had unfulfilled needs. Needs that Susan didn't seem inclined to acknowledge, and in truth, needs he wasn't sure she could have satisfied any longer even if she'd shown interest. Not with the distance between them, a gulf that had grown wider after Jack's birth. There were too many sleepless nights and grumpy mornings, too many laconic, grunted conversations in front of the television and not enough talking.

So Gary had gone elsewhere.

To Leila.

A crow called out above him, perched on a tree limb. The sound startled him, bringing Gary back to the present. The bird spread its wings and the branch bent under its wings. The leaves rustled as it took flight. Gary watched it go. His spirits plummeted even farther as the bird soared higher.

He stepped out from underneath the water tower's shadow, back into the sunlight, and shivered.

We beat the Martians, Daddy! Me and you, together...

"Oh Jack," he whispered, "I'm so sorry."

Gary felt eyes upon him, a tickling sensation between his shoulder blades. He glanced around. Through his tears, he noticed a rabbit at the edge of the field, watching him intently.

He sniffed, wiping his nose with the back of his hand.

The rabbit twitched its whiskers and kept staring. Gary felt its black eyes bore into him. He wondered if animals blinked.

The rabbit didn't.

"Scat." Gary stamped his foot. "Go on! Get out of here."

The rabbit scurried into the corn, vanishing as quickly as it had appeared. Gary studied the patch of grass where it had been sitting. The spot was empty, except for a large rock. Was it his imagination, or was the stone's surface red?

Maybe the animal was injured. Or dying.

His mind threatened to dredge up more of the past, and he bit his lip, drawing blood.

Gary checked the time on his cell phone. He'd been gone a long while. Susan would be worried. He shouldn't have left her alone, especially on today, of all days. But she'd insisted that at least one of them should visit Jack's grave. That was what had brought him here in the first place. He'd been drawn to the water tower without even thinking about it. Susan hadn't come with him to the cemetery. Said she couldn't bear it. She'd visited the grave many times over the past year, but not today. It had been left for Gary to do, and so he had.

He pressed a button, unlocking the keypad, and the phone's display lit up. It was just after twelve noon, on August fifteenth.

71

But he'd already known the date.

How could he forget?

He trudged back the way he'd come, wading through the sweltering afternoon haze. Heat waves shimmered in the corners of his vision.

He shouldn't have come here. Not today, on the one year anniversary of his son's death. This was a bad idea. It was bad enough that he could see this stupid water tower everywhere he went. Why come this close to it? What was he hoping to find? To prove?

The wind whispered, *Daddy.*

Gary turned around, and gasped.

Jack stood beneath the water tower, watching him go. The boy was dressed in the same clothes the police had found him in.

Daddy...

His son reached out. Jack was transparent. Gary could see corn stalks on the other side of him.

"No. Not real. You're not real."

La la la la, lemon. La la la la, lullaby...

Gary shivered. Jack's favorite song from *Sesame Street*. He'd sung it all the time. All about the letter 'L' and words that began with it; a Bert and Ernie classic from Gary's own childhood.

"You're not there," he told his son.

Gary stuck his pinky fingers in his ears and closed his eyes. When he opened them again, Jack was gone. He'd never been there. It was just the heat, playing tricks on him. He lowered his hands.

Something rustled between the rows of swaying corn.

Gary didn't believe in ghosts. He didn't need to. Memories could haunt a man much more than spirits ever could.

He walked home, passing through the cemetery on the way, and his son's grave.

He stopped at Jack's headstone, knelt in the grass, and wept. He did not see Jack again. He did spot several more rabbits, darting between tombstones, running through the grass. Playing amongst the dead.

He tried to ignore the fact that they all stopped to watch him pass.

By the time he got home, Gary's melancholy mood had turned into full-fledged depression. He'd been off the medication for months now, ever since he'd stopped seeing the counselor. If he went inside the house, he'd feel even worse. Susan had been crying all morning, looking at pictures of Jack. He couldn't deal with that right now. Couldn't handle her pain. He was supposed to fix things for them, and this couldn't be fixed. Gary couldn't stand to see her hurting. Had never been able to.

He decided to mow the lawn instead. Even though he dreaded mowing, sometimes it made him feel better—the aroma of fresh cut grass and the neat, symmetrical rows. He went into the garage; made sure the lawnmower had enough oil and gas, and then rolled it out into the yard. It started on the third tug.

Gary pushed the lawnmower up and down the yard and tried not to think. Grasshoppers and crickets jumped out of his way, and yellow dandelions disappeared beneath the blades. He'd completed five rows and was beginning his sixth when he noticed the baby bunny.

Or what was left of it.

The rabbit's upper half crawled through the yard, trailing viscera and blood, grass clippings sticking to its guts. Its lower body was missing, presumably pulped by the lawnmower. Gary's hands slipped off the safety bar, and the lawnmower dutifully turned itself off.

Silence descended, for a brief moment, and then he heard something else.

The baby rabbit made a noise, almost like a scream.

Daddy?

He glanced around, frantic. A few feet away, the grass moved. Something was underneath it, hiding beneath the surface. Gary walked over and bent down, parting the grass. His fingers came away sticky and red. Secreted inside the remains of their warren were four more baby bunnies. The lawnmower had mangled them, and they were dying as he watched. Their black eyes stared at him incriminatingly. The burrow was slick with gore and fur.

Gary turned away. His breakfast sprayed across the lawn.

Despite their injuries, despite missing limbs and dangling intestines, the bunnies continued to thrash, their movements weak and jerky.

"Oh God," he moaned. "Why don't they die? Why don't—"

The half-rabbit dragging itself across the yard squealed again.

"Please," Gary whimpered. "Just die. Don't do this. Not today. It's too much."

Daddy? Daddyyyy? La la la la, lemon. La la la la lullaby…

Gary stumbled to his feet and ran to the driveway. Without thinking, he seized the biggest rock he could find, dashed back to the rabbit hole, and raised the rock over his head.

"I'm sorry."

He flung it down as hard as he could, squashing them. Their tiny bones snapped like twigs underfoot. Swallowing hard, Gary picked the rock back up again, ignoring the sticky, matted blood and fur that now clung to its bottom and sides. He stalked across the yard, tracked down the half-bunny and put it out of its misery, too.

Gasping for breath, he let the rock lay in the grass, concealing the carcass. His bowels clenched; then loosened. Kneeling, he threw up again. When it was over, he washed his hands and face off beneath the outside spigot.

This time, the tears didn't stop.

Gary wailed. One of his neighbors poked their head outside, attracted by the ruckus. When they saw his face, saw the raw emotions etched onto it, they ducked back inside.

Eventually, when he'd gotten himself under control, Gary went inside. He poured a double scotch, and gulped it down. The liquor burned his raw throat. He called out for Susan, but there was no answer. He found her in Jack's bedroom, sitting on their son's bed and holding one of his action figures. Her face was wet and pale. He sat down next to her, put his arm around her, and they cried together for a long time.

That night, Susan said she'd like to try again; she'd like to have another child. She murmured in his ear that it had been a long time since they'd made love, and apologized for it. Said it was her fault, and she'd like to try and fix things. Make them like they used to be, long ago, when they'd first been married. Every party of Gary stiffened, except for the part of him that could have helped insure that. When she noticed, and asked what was wrong, he told her that he didn't feel good. Too depressed. Susan pulled away. She asked Gary if he still loved her and he lied and said yes. She snuggled closer again, and put her head on his chest.

Gary thought of Leila and tried very hard not to scream. The guilt was a solid thing, and it weighed on him heavier than the thick blankets pulled over his body. He held Susan until she fell asleep and then he slipped out from underneath her. She moaned in her sleep, a sad sound. He went downstairs, turned on the television, and curled into the fetal position on the couch.

He'd never told her about Leila. As far as he knew, Susan had never expected. At one point, he'd thought the secret might come out. Leila had made threats. She was unhappy. Wanted Gary to leave Susan and be with her. He'd been worried, frantic—unsure of what to do. But then Jack had died and the whole affair had become moot. For the past year, he and Susan had both been overwhelmed with grief. And though Leila was no longer in the picture, and though Gary had tried very hard to be there for his wife and make the marriage work, he couldn't tell Susan now. She was a mother who'd lost her child.

He couldn't hurt her all over again.

Restless, Gary tossed and turned. The couch springs squeaked. Eventually, he needed to pee. Rather than using the upstairs bathroom and risk waking Susan, he went outside, into the backyard. He pushed his robe aside, fumbled with the fly on his pajamas, and unleashed a stream.

And then he froze.

In the darkness, a pair of shiny little eyes stared back at him. Although he couldn't see the animal itself, Gary knew what it was—the mother rabbit, looking for her dead children.

"I'm sorry," he whispered.

The eyes vanished in the darkness.

He went back inside and lay down on the couch again. Sleep would not come, nor would relief from the pain. It hadn't been this bad in a while, not since the months immediately following Jack's death.

Gary stared at the television without seeing.

It was a long time before he slept.

That December, when Gary got home from a particularly harrowing day at the office, Susan was in the bedroom, holding the stick from a home pregnancy test. It was the second of the day. She'd taken the first that morning, after he left for work. Both showed positive; a little blue plus sign, simple in its symbolism, yet powerful as well. That tiny plus sign led to joy and happiness—or sometimes—fear and heartbreak.

Susan was ecstatic, and that night, after they'd eaten a romantic, candlelight dinner, and curled up together to watch a movie, and made love, Gary decided that he'd never tell her about Leila. Not now. He couldn't.

After all, he'd lived with the guilt this long.

He could do it for the rest of his life.

According to the obstetrician, (an asthmatic, paunchy man named Doctor Brice) Susan was due in August, within ten days of the anniversary of Jack's death.

On the way home from Doctor Brice's office, Susan turned to Gary.

"It's a sign."

"What is?"

"My due date. It's like a sign from God."

Gary kept silent. He thought it might be the exact opposite.

Two years later.

On the second anniversary of their son's death, with Susan's due date a little more than a week away, they woke up, dressed solemnly, and prepared to visit Jack's grave. Susan had picked a floral arrangement the night before, and both of them had taken the day off work.

Once again, the August heat and humidity was insufferable. Gary waded through the thick miasma on his way to start the car (so that the air conditioner would have time to cool the interior before Susan came out). He slipped behind the wheel, put the key in the ignition, and turned it. The car sputtered and then something exploded. There was a horrible screech, followed by a wet thump. The engine hissed, and a brief gust of steam or smoke billowed from beneath the hood.

Cursing, Gary yanked on the hood release and jumped out of the car. He ran around to the front, popped the hood, and raised it. The stench was awful. He stumbled backward. Something wet and red had splattered all over the engine. Tufts of brown and white fur stuck to the metal. A disembodied foot lay on top of the battery.

A rabbit's foot.

Guess he wasn't so lucky, Gary thought, biting back a giggle. He was horrified, but at the same time, overwhelmed with the bizarre desire to laugh.

The rabbit must have crawled up into the engine block overnight, perhaps seeking warmth or just looking for a place to nest. When Gary had started the car, the animal most likely panicked and scurried for cover, taking a fatal misstep into the whirring fan blades.

He glanced back down at the severed rabbit's foot again.

A bunny. Same day. Just like last year. With the lawnmower. He'd run over the nest, and then he'd… with the rock…

Susan tapped him on the shoulder and he nearly screamed. When she saw the mess beneath the hood, she almost did the same.

"What happened?"

"A rabbit. It must have crawled inside last night."

She recoiled, one hand covering her mouth. "Oh, that's terrible. The poor thing."

"Yeah. Let me get this cleaned up and then we'll go."

Susan began to sob. Gary went to her, and she sagged against him.

"I'm sorry. It's just…"

"I know," Gary consoled her. "I know."

She pushed away. "I think I'm going to be sick."

"Susan—"

Turning, she waddled as quickly as she could back to the house. Gary followed her, heard her retching in the bathroom, and after a moment's hesitation, knocked gently on the door.

"You okay?"

"No," she choked. "I don't think I can go. You'll go without me?"

"But Susan, I…"

She retched again. Gary closed his eyes.

"Please, Gary? I can't go. Not like this. One of us has to."

"You're right, of course."

Susan heard the reluctance in his voice.

"Please?"

Gary sighed. "Will you be okay?"

The toilet flushed. "Yes. I just need to rest. Remember to take the flowers."

"I will. Susan?"

"What?"

"I'm sorry."

He heard her running water in the sink.

"Don't be sorry," she said. "It's not your fault."

The graveyard was empty, except for an elderly couple on their way out as Gary arrived. Despite the heat, he'd decided to walk to the cemetery rather than dealing with the mess beneath the hood of his car. By the time he reached Jack's grave he was drenched in sweat, his clothing soaked.

Panting, he knelt in front of the grave. Droplets of perspiration ran into his eyes, stinging them. His vision blurred, and then the tears began. They were false tears, crocodile tears, tears of sweat and exertion, rather than grief. Oh, the grief was there. Gary was overwhelmed with grief. Grief was a big lump that sat in his throat. But still, the real tears would not come.

But the memories did.

When he glanced up at the water tower, the memories came full force.

Grief turned to guilt.

"I mean it, Gary. I'm telling Susan."

"You'll do no such thing."

Leila's smile was tight-lipped, almost a grimace. "I've got her email address."

Gary paused. Felt fear. "You're lying."

"Try me." Now her smile was genuine again, if cruel. "I looked it up on the internet. From her company's website."

Gary sighed. "Why? Why do this to me?"

"Because I'm sick of your bullshit. You said you loved me. You said you'd leave her—"

"I've told you, it's not that simple. I've got to think about Jack."

"She can't take Jack from you. You're his father. You've got rights."

"I can't take that chance. Damn it, Leila, we've been through this a million times. I love you, but I—"

"You're a fucking liar, Gary! Just stop it. If you loved me, you'd tell her."

"I do love you."

"Then do it. Tell her. If you don't have the balls to, I will."

"Are you threatening me? You gonna blackmail me into continuing this? Is that it?"

"If I have to."

Gary wasn't sure what happened next. They'd been naked, sitting side by side on the blanket, their fluids drying on each other's body, the water tower's shadow protecting them from the warm afternoon sun, hiding their illicit tryst. He wasn't aware that he was straddling Leila until his hands curled around her throat.

Choking, she lashed out at him. Her long, red fingernails raked across his naked chest. Flailing blindly, his hand closed around the rock. He raised it over his head and Leila's eyes grew large.

"Gary…"

The rock smashed into her mouth, cutting off the rest.

He lost all control then, hammering her face and head repeatedly. He blocked out everything; her screams, the frightened birds taking flight, his own nonsensical curses. Everything—until he heard the singing.

"La la la la, lemon. La la la la lullaby…"

Jack. Singing his favorite song.

The boy stepped into the clearing. Believing his father was working that Saturday (because that was the lie Gary had told Susan and Jack so that he could meet up with Leila for an afternoon quickie in the first place—he'd even stayed logged into his computer at work so that if anybody checked, it would look like he was there working), Jack froze in mid-melody, a mixture of puzzlement and terror on his face.

"Daddy?"

"Jack!"

His son turned and ran. Jack sprang to his feet, naked and bloody, and chased after him.

"Jack, stop! Daddy can explain."

"Mommy…"

Unaware that he was still holding the rock, until he struck his son in the back of the head.

"I said stop!"

Jack toppled face first into the grass. He did not move. Did not breathe.

When Gary checked his pulse, he had none.

Something inside Gary shut itself off at that moment.

The rest of the memories became a blur. He dressed. Wrapped the blanket around Leila and loaded her into the trunk of the car, which he'd parked behind the abandoned strip mall, just beyond the cemetery and the water tower. Her blood hadn't yet seeped out onto the grass, and he made sure none of her teeth or any shreds of tissue were in sight. He'd thrown her clothes and purse inside the car as well.

Then he picked up the bloody rock, the rock that he'd just bludgeoned his son to death with, and threw it down a nearby rabbit hole.

He drove to the edge of LeHorn's Hollow, where a sinkhole had opened up the summer before, and dumped Leila's body. Gary knew that the local farmers sometimes dumped their dead livestock in the same hole, as did hunters after field dressing wild game. The chances were good that she'd never be found.

He cleaned his hands off in a nearby stream, then got back in the car and drove to the closest convenience store. He bought some cleaning supplies, paid cash, and then found a secluded spot where he could clean out the trunk. Then he returned to the office, unlocked the door, logged himself off the computer, and went home.

Then he went home.

The police knocked on the door a few hours later. Three teenaged boys found Jack's body. One of them, Seth Ferguson (who was no stranger to juvenile detention) immediately fell under suspicion. When the police cleared him later that day, they questioned the local registered sex offenders, even though Jack's body had shown no signs of sexual abuse. In the weeks and months that followed, there were no new leads. The case was never solved.

The murder weapon was never found.

Daddy...

Gary sat up and wiped his eyes. Steadying himself on his son's tombstone, he clambered to his feet. His joints popped. He hadn't aged well in the last two years, and his body was developing the ailments of a man twice his age, arthritis being one of them.

Daddy?

"Oh Jack," Gary whispered. "Why couldn't you have stayed home that day?"

Daddy...

His son's voice grew louder, calling to him, pleading. Sad. Lonely.

Slowly, like a marionette on strings, Gary shuffled towards the water tower.

"Where are you, Jack? Show me. Tell me what I have to do to make it up to you."

Daddy... Daddy... Daddy...

The voice was right next to him. Gary looked around, fully expecting to see his son's ghost, but instead, he spied the rabbits. A dozen or so bunnies formed a loose circle around the water tower. They'd been silent, and had appeared as if from nowhere.

Penning him in.

Daddy. Down here.

Gary looked down at the ground.

Jack's voice echoed from inside a rabbit hole.

The same hole he'd thrown the rock into.

Gary's skin prickled. Despite his fear, he leaned over and

81

stared into the hole. There was a flurry of movement inside, and then a rabbit darted out and joined the others. Then another. Whimpering, Gary stepped backward. More bunnies poured themselves from the earth, and he felt their eyes on him—accusing.

Condemning.

"What do you want?"

Daddy.

Gary screamed.

They found him when the sun went down. He'd screamed himself hoarse while pawing at the ground around his son's grave. His fingers were dirty, and several of his fingernails were bloody and ragged, hanging by thin strands of tissue. He babbled about bunnies, but no one could understand him. The police arrived, as did an ambulance.

From the undergrowth, a brown bunny rabbit watched them load Gary into the ambulance.

When he was gone, it hopped away.

This story first appeared on the Horror World *website, and was reprinted in my out-of-print short story collection* Unhappy Endings. *It takes place in the same town as my novels* Dark Hollow *and* Ghost Walk *(as does the end of* Take The Long Way Home *and several other short stories), and alert readers might recognize a few familiar places and people. The water tower exists much as I described it here, but it is far less sinister in real life. My oldest son and I used to play there when he was little. The mishap with the rabbits and the lawnmower is also based on something that happened in real life. I was mowing my lawn and accidentally hit a hidden nest of baby rabbits. It was horrifying and terrible and I felt guilty about it for months afterward. I channeled some of that into the story.*

THAT WHICH
LINGERS

Sarah awoke to the wailing alarm clock. Blurry-eyed and still half asleep, she went for her morning run—from the bedroom to the bathroom. Three seconds later, she knelt, retching as she'd done every morning for the past two months.

Finished, she collapsed onto the couch and lit the day's first cigarette while the coffee brewed. A dull ache behind her temples was all that remained from the night before. Sarah frowned, trying to recall the exact details. She remembered arguing with the bartender. He hadn't wanted to serve her, commenting on her *condition*. After some flirting, she'd managed to hook up with several men who were willing to buy a girl a drink in exchange for a hint of things to come.

At least she hadn't gotten completely smashed and ended up bringing one of them home. Her empty bed testified to that. She hadn't shared it since Christopher walked out on her four months ago. She inhaled, letting the acrid smoke fill her lungs, and fought back tears.

Sarah showered, trying to wake up as the water caressed her skin. Trying to lose herself in a flood of happy thoughts. Trying not to notice the swell of her abdomen as she lathered her lower body. Trying to cope.

She wrapped her long, chestnut hair in a towel, and cinched another around her waist. Then she grabbed breakfast. The coffee was good, but a single bite of the granola bar made her stomach nauseous again.

She let the towels drop to the floor and caught a glimpse of herself in the mirror. This too, reminded her of Christopher.

They'd dated for three years. The pregnancy had been unplanned. Christopher had been ecstatic—and crushed when he learned that she didn't feel the same way. She'd tried to explain how she felt. How the timing wasn't right. She still wanted to go back to school and get her bachelor's degree. She wanted to do more with her life than working as a waitress. Having a baby now would jeopardize all of that.

What she hadn't told him was that she worried about his drinking and of how he was turning out to be just like the father he hated. She didn't express that she had come to seriously doubt their relationship.

Christopher was completely opposed to the abortion.

Sarah noticed how her breasts were growing fuller while echoes of Christopher's pleas rang in her ears.

The abortion had devastated him, killing whatever chance of love they'd still had. A part of both of them had died that day.

That was four months ago.

Collapsing onto the unmade bed, she began to cry. How could she possibly deal with what was happening to her alone? She needed Christopher.

She'd considered having an ultrasound, but knew that nothing would show up during the procedure.

She wasn't crazy.

She was haunted.

Deep inside, Sarah felt something kick.

The original version of this story appeared in my very first short story collection, No Rest For the Wicked, *which is long out-of-print. I touched it up a bit for its appearance in* A Little Silver Book of Streetwise Stories *(also out of print), but left most of it intact. This is one of the first short stories I ever sold for publication, and it remains a personal favorite. When it was first published, it caused a minor stir on early internet message boards among both pro-life and anti-abortion readers. That surprised me at the time, but the internet was young and new then, and things like flame wars and trolls hadn't been invented yet. Rest assured, I had no political agenda with this tale. I just thought it was a pretty cool ghost story.*

TWO-HEADED ALIEN LOVE CHILD

Kaine worked for the government. This was not something he revealed when meeting women or starting conversations. These days, with all of the paranoia and conspiracy theories, it was best to keep silent. When meeting women and starting conversations, Kaine introduced himself as an appliance salesman from New Jersey.

He'd served the department for thirty years, watching it grow from a tiny office into a sprawling bureaucratic monstrosity with buildings in every city of every state. He'd watched administrations rise and fall, witnessed cover-ups and exposures. He'd seen other divisions like the CIA and NSA hide their tracks repeatedly, but his division had *never* been covert. It worked with and among the civilians it was designed to help. True, in recent decades it had become slower and less efficient, but it still never failed to get the job done.

Getting the job done was something Kaine took very seriously. That was why he sat here tonight, listening to Neil Diamond while the rain beat upon the roof of his non-descript sedan. Sitting on a quiet suburban street in Idaho. Sitting outside the home of Sylvia Burns, a woman who, like thousands of young, unwed, or divorced mothers before her, was burdened by evil.

A blinding flash burst silently above the house like a miniature sunrise. Kaine glanced at the dashboard clock. *12:47 a.m.* Right on schedule. Then the clock flashed zeros as 'Sweet Caroline' dissolved into static. Outside, the streetlights dimmed, plunging the housing development into darkness. Kaine knew from experience that the neighbors would sleep undisturbed throughout the occurrence.

A ball of light appeared, soaring down from the sky and hovering just off the ground. A ramp descended and six diminutive figures walked out of the sphere. They approached Sylvia's bedroom window, and vanished into the house. After a few minutes, they reappeared, carrying a comatose Sylvia between them. The gray-skinned beings disappeared into the craft. The ramp began to recede.

Pausing only to smooth his tie, Kaine crept through the darkness, clutching an unregistered semiautomatic pistol in one hand, and a black briefcase in the other. Swiftly, he leapt onto the platform. The figures had retreated into the depths of the vessel. Kaine shuddered as he recalled Sylvia's description of the craft's interior.

The hatch closed behind him. Kaine examined the dimly lit corridor. A distant humming reverberated off the walls and floor. A bluish-green glow emanated from a doorway at the end of the hall. He examined the strange symbols scrawled across the door. Kaine placed the briefcase at his feet and touched the cold metal. It throbbed from deep inside, as if it were a living thing. Seconds later, the door slid open, revealing a nightmarish scene.

His client lay naked on a table, surrounded by dozens of the alien beings. They were vaguely humanoid, with two arms and two legs, but their heads were much larger than the rest of their bodies and their eyes were huge, dwarfing their almost nonexistent noses and mouths.

Kaine had seen them before. His mind flashed back to a supermarket tabloid from ten months ago: **WOMAN IMPREGNATED BY ALIEN ABDUCTORS.** Beneath the garish headline had been a photograph of Sylvia. Two weeks later, Kaine became her caseworker.

"Nobody move." He raised the pistol with one hand and unlatched the briefcase with his other. Kaine pulled a stack of papers out of the briefcase. The aliens cringed, fear flashing in their black eyes. Kaine held a document before him like a shield. "My name is Kaine. I am a Domestic Relations Officer, as well as the caseworker for the young woman you have strapped to that table."

He flung the paperwork toward the tightly clustered aliens, and undid Sylvia's straps. She clung to him weakly, as if waking from a dream.

"This, gentlemen, is a court order for child support. You are hereby ordered to appear in domestic court one month from today for a child support hearing. My client claims that you impregnated her; therefore, you are financially responsible for part of the child's welfare. Bring whatever pay stubs and supporting documents you may have with you. Also bring a copy of your most recent tax return. If you can not afford an attorney, one will be appointed to you by the state."

Still brandishing the gun, Kaine backed Sylvia towards the exit.

"The next time you decide to abduct and impregnate someone in my state, gentlemen, I suggest you remember that we do not go lightly on deadbeat dads. Good evening to you."

The door hissed shut behind them, leaving the aliens to stare at one another in bewilderment.

"Shit," said one. "We haven't fucked up this bad since Roswell."

The original version of this story appeared in my first short story collection, No Rest For the Wicked *(which is long out-of-print). I revised it considerably for its appearance in* A Little Silver Book of Streetwise Stories. *I'm not sure where I got the idea. I think it stemmed from drinking a six-pack of beer while watching* The X-Files.

GOLDEN BOY

I shit gold.

It started around the time I hit puberty. I thought there was something wrong with me. Cancer or parasites or something like that, because when I looked down into the bowl, a golden turd was sitting on the bottom. When I wiped, there were gold stains on the toilet paper. Then I flushed and went back to watching cartoons. Ten minutes later, I'd forgotten all about it.

You know how kids are.

But it wasn't just my shit. I pissed gold. (No golden showers jokes, please. I've heard them all before). I started sweating gold. It oozed out of my pores in little droplets, drying on my skin in flakes. It peeled off easily enough. Just like dead skin after a bad case of sunburn. Then my spit and mucous started turning into gold. I'd hock gold nuggets onto the sidewalk. One day, I was picking mulberries from a tree in a pasture. There was a barbed-wire fence beneath the tree, and to reach the higher branches, I stood on the fence. I lost my balance and the barbed-wire took three big chunks out of the back of my thigh. My blood was liquid gold. And like I said, this was around puberty, so you can only imagine what my wet dreams were like. Many nights, instead of waking up wet and sticky, I woke up with a hard, metallic mess on my sheets and in my pajamas.

Understand, my bodily fluids weren't just gold colored. If they had been, things might have turned out differently. But they were actual gold—that precious metal coveted all over the world. Gold—the source of wars and peace, the rise of empires and their eventual collapse, murders and robberies, wealth and poverty, love and hate.

My parents figured it out soon enough. So did the first doctor they took me to. Oh, yeah. That doctor was very interested. He wanted to keep me for observation. Wanted to conduct some more tests. He said all this with his doctor voice but you could see the greed in his eyes.

And he was just the first.

Mom and Dad weren't having any of that. They took me home and told me this was going to be our little secret. I was special. I had a gift from God. A wonderful, magnificent talent—but one that might be misunderstood by others. They wanted to help me avoid that, they said. Didn't want me to be made fun of or taken advantage of. Even now, I honestly think they meant it at the time. They believed that their intentions were for the best. But you know what they say about good intentions. The road to hell is paved with them. That's bullshit, of course.

The road to hell is paved with fucking gold.

My parents started skimming my residue. Mom scraped gold dust from my clothes and the sheets when she did laundry and from the rim of my glass after dinner. One night, they told me I couldn't watch my favorite TV show because I wouldn't eat my broccoli. I cried gold tears. After that, it seemed like they made me cry a lot.

Everywhere I went, I left a trail of gold behind me. My parents collected it, invested it, and soon, we moved to a bigger house in a nicer neighborhood with a better school. Our family of three grew. We had a maid and a cook and groundskeepers.

I hated it, at first. The new house was too big. We'd been a blue-collar family. Now, Mom and Dad didn't work anymore and I suddenly found myself thrown into classrooms with a bunch of snobby rich kids—all because of my gift. I had nothing in common with my classmates. They talked about books and music that I'd never heard of, and argued politics and civic responsibilities and French Impressionism. They idolized Che Guevara and Ayn Rand and Ernest Hemingway. I read comic books and listened to hip-hop and liked Spider-Man.

So I tried to fit in. Nobody wants to be hated. It's human nature—wanting to be liked by your peers. Soon enough, I found a way. I let them in on my little secret. Within a week, I was the most popular kid in school. I had more friends than I knew what to do with. Everybody wanted to be friends with the golden boy. But here's the thing. They didn't want to be friends with me because of who I was. They wanted to be friends with me because of *who* I was. There's a big difference between those two things.

So I had friends. Girlfriends, too.

I remember the first girl I ever loved. She was beautiful. There's nothing as powerful or pure or unstable as first love. I thought about her constantly. Stared at her in class. Dreamed of her at night. And when she returned my interest, my body felt like a coiled spring. It was the happiest day of my life. But she didn't love me for who I was. Like everyone else, she loved me for *who* I was.

So have all the rest. Both ex-wives and the string of long-term girlfriends between them. My happiest relationships are one night stands. The only women I'm truly comfortable with are the ones I only know for a few brief hours. I never tell them who I am or what I can do. And before you ask, yes, I always wear a condom and no, I can't have children. There are no little golden boys in my future. I don't shoot blanks. I shoot bullets.

I've no shortage of job opportunities. Banks, financial groups, precious metals dealers, jewelers, even several governments. Of course, I don't need to work. I can live off my talent for the rest of my life. So can everyone else around me. But that doesn't stop the employment offers from coming. And they're so insincere and patronizing. So very fucking patronizing. They want to invest in my future. Just like my parents and my friends and my wives, they only want what's best for me. Or so they claim.

But I know what they really want.

And I can't take it anymore.

I'm spent. My gold is tarnished. It's lost its gleam. Its shine. I can see it, and I wonder if others are noticing, too.

Here's what's going to happen. I'm going to put this gun to my head and blow my brains out all over the room, leaving a golden spray pattern on the wall. The medical examiner will pick skull fragments and gold nuggets out of the plaster. The mortician can line his pockets before embalming me. You can sell my remains on eBay, and invest in them, and fight over what's left.

I want to fade away, but gold never fades. This is my gift. This is my legacy. This is my curse.

I have only one thing to leave behind.

You can spend me when I'm gone.

This story first appeared in A Little Silver Book of Streetwise Stories. *The first and last sentences came to me one day, and I liked them so much that I wrote a story to tie them together. A friend of mine, fellow writer Kelli Owen, read this prior to publication and said it was a metaphor for my current place in the genre. But Kelli is quite possibly mentally ill, and says that about all of my work. Plus, I'm fairly certain she was drunk when she read it. Take from "Golden Boy" what you will, but I just think it's a quirky and kind of fun fable. Not a metaphor, and (hopefully) not a prediction of the future.*

BRIAN KEENE is the author of over twenty-five books, including *Darkness on the Edge of Town, Urban Gothic, Castaways, Kill Whitey, Dark Hollow, Dead Sea, Ghoul* and *The Rising*. He also writes comic books such as *The Last Zombie, Doom Patrol* and *Dead of Night: Devil Slayer*. His work has been translated into German, Spanish, Polish, Italian, French and Taiwanese. Several of his novels and stories have been optioned for film, one of which, *The Ties That Bind*, premiered on DVD in 2009 as a critically-acclaimed independent short. Keene's work has been praised in such diverse places as *The New York Times*, The History Channel, The Howard Stern Show, CNN.com, *Publisher's Weekly, Fangoria Magazine*, and *Rue Morgue Magazine*. Keene lives in Central Pennsylvania. You can communicate with him online at www.briankeene.com, on Facebook at www.facebook.com/pages/Brian-Keene/189077221397 or on Twitter at www.twitter.com/BrianKeene

deadite press

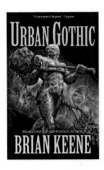

"Urban Gothic" Brian Keene - When their car broke down in a dangerous inner-city neighborhood, Kerri and her friends thought they would find shelter inside an old, dark row home. They thought they would be safe there until help arrived. They were wrong. The residents who live down in the cellar and the tunnels beneath the city are far more dangerous than the streets outside, and they have a very special way of dealing with trespassers. Trapped in a world of darkness, populated by obscene abominations, they will have to fight back if they ever want to see the sun again.

"Jack's Magic Beans" Brian Keene - It happens in a split-second. One moment, customers are happily shopping in the Save-A-Lot grocery store. The next instant, they are transformed into bloodthirsty psychotics, interested only in slaughtering one another and committing unimaginably atrocious and frenzied acts of violent depravity. Deadite Press is proud to bring one of Brian Keene's bleakest and most violent novellas back into print once more. This edition also includes four bonus short stories.

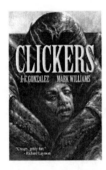

"Clickers" J. F. Gonzalez and Mark Williams- They are the Clickers, giant venomous blood-thirsty crabs from the depths of the sea. The only warning to their rampage of dismemberment and death is the terrible clicking of their claws. But these monsters aren't merely here to ravage and pillage. They are being driven onto land by fear. Something is hunting the Clickers. Something ancient and without mercy. *Clickers* is J. F. Gonzalez and Mark Williams' gore-soaked cult classic tribute to the giant monster B-movies of yesteryear.

"Clickers II" J. F. Gonzalez and Brian Keene- Thousands of Clickers swarm across the entire nation and march inland, slaughtering anyone and anything they come across. But this time the Clickers aren't blindly rushing onto land - they are being led by an intelligence older than civilization itself. A force that wants to take dry land away from the mammals. Those left alive soon realize that they must do everything and anything they can to protect humanity – no matter the cost. *This isn't war, this is extermination.*

"A Gathering of Crows" Brian Keene - Five mysterious figures are about to pay a visit to Brinkley Springs. They have existed for centuries, emerging from the shadows only to destroy. To kill. To feed. They bring terror and carnage, and leave blood and death in their wake. The only person that can prevent their rampage is ex-Amish magus Levi Stoltzfus. As the night wears on, Brinkley Springs will be quiet no longer. Screams will break the silence. But when the sun rises again, will there be anyone left alive to hear?

"Take the Long Way Home" Brian Keene - All across the world, people suddenly vanish in the blink of an eye. Gone. Steve, Charlie and Frank were just trying to get home when it happened. Trapped in the ultimate traffic jam, they watch as civilization collapses, claiming the souls of those around them. God has called his faithful home, but the invitations for Steve, Charlie and Frank got lost. Now they must set off on foot through a nightmarish post-apocalyptic landscape in search of answers. In search of God. In search of their loved ones. And in search of home.

"Brain Cheese Buffet" Edward Lee - collecting nine of Lee's most sought after tales of violence and body fluids. Featuring the Stoker nominated "Mr. Torso," the legendary gross-out piece "The Dritiphilist," the notorious "The McCrath Model SS40-C, Series S," and six more stories to test your gag reflex.
"Edward Lee's writing is fast and mean as a chain saw revved to full-tilt boogie."
  - Jack Ketchum

"Bullet Through Your Face" Edward Lee - No writer is more extreme, perverted, or gross than Edward Lee. His world is one of psychopathic redneck rapists, sex addicted demons, and semen stealing aliens. Brace yourself, the king of splatterspunk is guaranteed to shock, offend, and make you laugh until you vomit.
"Lee pulls no punches."
  - Fangoria

THE VERY BEST IN CULT HORROR

deadite
press

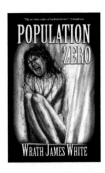

"Population Zero" Wrath James White - An intense sadistic tale of how one man will save the world through sterilization. *Population Zero* is the story of an environmental activist named Todd Hammerstein who is on a mission to save the planet. In just 50 years the population of the planet is expected to double. But not if Todd can help it. From Wrath James White, the celebrated master of sex and splatter, comes a tale of environmentalism, drugs, and genital mutilation.

"Trolley No. 1852" Edward Lee - In 1934, horror writer H.P. Lovecraft is invited to write a story for a subversive underground magazine, all on the condition that a pseudonym will be used. The pay is lofty, and God knows, Lovecraft needs the money. There's just one catch. It has to be a pornographic story . . . The 1852 Club is a bordello unlike any other. Its women are the most beautiful and they will do anything. But there is something else going on at this sex club. In the back rooms monsters are performing vile acts on each other and doors to other dimensions are opening . . .

"Zombies and Shit" Carlton Mellick III - *Battle Royale* meets *Return of the Living Dead* in this post-apocalyptic action adventure. Twenty people wake to find themselves in a boarded-up building in the middle of the zombie wasteland. They soon realize they have been chosen as contestants on a popular reality show called Zombie Survival. Each contestant is given a backpack of supplies and a unique weapon. Their goal: be the first to make it through the zombie-plagued city to the pick-up zone alive. A campy, trashy, punk rock gore fest.

"Slaughterhouse High" Robert Devereaux - It's prom night in the Demented States of America. A place where schools are built with secret passageways, rebellious teens get zippers installed in their mouths and genitals, and once a year one couple is slaughtered and the bits of their bodies are kept as souvenirs. But something's gone terribly wrong when the secret killer starts claiming a far higher body count than usual . . .
"A major talent!" - Poppy Z. Brite

"The Book of a Thousand Sins" Wrath James White - Welcome to a world of Zombie nymphomaniacs, psychopathic deities, voodoo surgery, and murderous priests. Where mutilation sex clubs are in vogue and torture machines are sex toys. No one makes it out alive – not even God himself.

"If Wrath James White doesn't make you cringe, you must be riding in the wrong end of a hearse."
-Jack Ketchum

"The Haunter of the Threshold" Edward Lee - There is something very wrong with this backwater town. Suicide notes, magic gems, and haunted cabins await her. Plus the woods are filled with monsters, both human and otherworldly. And then there are the horrible tentacles . . . Soon Hazel is thrown into a battle for her life that will test her sanity and sex drive. The sequel to H.P. Lovecraft's The Haunter of the Dark is Edward Lee's most pornographic novel to date!

"Apeshit" Carlton Mellick III - Friday the 13th meets Visitor Q. Six hipster teens go to a cabin in the woods inhabited by a deformed killer. An incredibly fucked-up parody of B-horror movies with a bizarro slant
"The new gold standard in unstoppable fetus-fucking kill-freakomania . . . Genuine all-meat hardcore horror meets unadulterated Bizarro brainwarp strangeness. The results are beyond jaw-dropping, and fill me with pure, unforgivable joy." - John Skipp

"Super Fetus" Adam Pepper - Try to abort this fetus and he'll kick your ass!
"The story of a self-aware fetus whose morally bankrupt mother is desperately trying to abort him. This darkly humorous novella will surely appall and upset a sizable percentage of people who read it . . . In-your-face, allegorical social commentary."
- BarnesandNoble.com

AVAILABLE FROM AMAZON.COM

235357LV00010B/192/P

9 781936 383559